THE LOVE LETTERS TO AMELIA

MAGGIE MEDINA

Copyright © 2025 MARIA M. MEDINA

All rights reserved

The characters and events portrayed in this book are fictitious. Any similarity to real persons, living or dead, is coincidental and not intended by the author.

No part of this book may be reproduced, or stored in a retrieval system, or transmitted in any form or by any means, electronic, mechanical, photocopying, recording, or otherwise, without express written permission of the publisher.

ISBN-13: 9798307506059

Cover design by: Art Painter
Library of Congress Control Number: 2018675309
Printed in the United States of America

I dedicate this book to my parents, Ramon and Elena Medina. Their 42 years of marriage, love, family, dedication, passion, and adventure taught us to live our lives the same way. I miss them very much.

CONTENTS

Title Page
Copyright
Dedication
Introduction

CHAPTER 1	1
CHAPTER 2	6
CHAPTER 3	11
CHAPTER 4	30
CHAPTER 5	38
CHAPTER 6	43
CHAPTER 7	46
CHAPTER 8	50
CHAPTER 9	52
CHAPTER 10	56
CHAPTER 11	60
CHAPTER 12	73
CHAPTER 13	76
CHAPTER 14	82
CHAPTER 15	92
CHAPTER 16	97
CHAPTER 17	100

CHAPTER 18	104
CHAPTER 19	109
THE LOVE LETTERS	111
The Love Letter From	114
The Love Letter from	115
THANK YOU	116

INTRODUCTION

The Love Letters is a book about a woman, Amelia, who suffers in her brief marriage and disturbing divorce. Then she begins to receive letters in the mail.

Beginning simple and becoming more and more descriptive, she is intrigued at first and then falls in love with the writer. She comes to realize that the **"heart wants what the heart wants!"**

Love and passion do not necessarily come when you are face-to-face. They can be mythical and magical, the heart and mind combining to make love and passion come to life.

In the end, all humans crave love. It is just human nature.

CHAPTER 1

Amelia opened the front door and walked slowly to the mailbox. She felt the chilly wind that blew against her body and seemed to go through her fleece jacket. It sent a shiver up her body.

She saw the trees swaying in the breeze and heard the rustle of the leaves and branches made as they moved. She noticed the cars in her neighbor's driveway, knowing family members were visiting old Mrs. Bryant, as she was getting up in age. Amelia saddened slightly, because she was such a nice lady, and called Amelia every day to check on her.

Amelia opened the black mailbox, reached in, and pulled out a red envelope. It was addressed to her but appeared to have no return address. She flipped it over, and there was nothing on the back. She noticed the beautiful rose stamp on the front, and postmark from her hometown, Charleston, South Carolina.

She put the envelope in her jacket pocket. Amelia slowly walked back into her small house and didn't give the envelope another thought. She entered the house and began to think about what she wanted for dinner.

She sauntered through the house and into the kitchen, opened the refrigerator, then the pantry to start taking things out to fix. She settled on vegetable soup, and gathered the items she would need. A bag of frozen veggies from the refrigerator, a quart of chicken broth and canned tomatoes from the pantry, a packet of French onion soup mix from the spice cabinet, and finally, her beloved red soup pot. The pot held a special place in Amelia's heart, as it had been her grandmothers, then her mothers. Now it was hers.

Putting the ingredients into the pot, she added a little sea salt and black pepper to taste, covered the pot and let it simmer. It would be an hour before the soup would be ready; just enough time for her to check her email and watch a little television.

She was glad she was off work, so she could watch her favorite television shows, or read one of her new books. She had never had the time before. She had been married and worked; then had been controlled and suffered at the hands of her ex-husband.

She would never forget what she had been through two years ago. Her short marriage to Mark had started ideally and ended horrifically. Her thoughts kept going back to that final day...the day she had ended up in the hospital. That fateful day when she almost died, had allowed her to gain her freedom.

She and Mark had argued because she had forgotten to go to the grocery store on the way home. The items she forgot were what he wanted her to fix for dinner. When he questioned her and called her "good for nothing" and a few other choice things, she knew this was not a regular argument. In a fit of rage, he grabbed her by the throat, she screamed loudly, but he continued to choke her until she was unconscious. When she finally opened her eyes, she was on a gurney being put into an ambulance, and Mark was under arrest.

Thank God for good old Mrs. Bryant. She had heard the scream and called the police. They arrived within seconds after she had gone unconscious. His handprint still visible on her throat. The detectives had come after the police, taken statements, completed an investigation, then had charged Mark with attempted murder, and first-degree assault.

At the hospital she was checked out by doctors, then ordered to have respiratory treatments every 4 hours to make sure her swollen throat didn't restrict her breathing. She was relieved since it could have been worse.

The doctors cleared her to give a statement, so Amelia spoke with the detectives. They had already talked to Mrs. Bryant and taken pictures of her neck. They informed Amelia that the evidence was damning, and believed Mark would be found guilty as charged.

Amelia's emotions gave way, and she began to cry. Her nightmare would soon be over. The marriage she had hoped would be loving and happy would soon cease to exist. She cried and breathed a sigh of relief.

Doctors had decided to keep her for several days, after the police had taken her statement. The nurses then took over and made her comfortable in a private room. The respiratory treatments continued too.

Her mind and body felt such relief and desperate sadness at the same time. She continued to cry throughout the night until she fell asleep from exhaustion.

Hours later, the sun coming through the hospital window awakened Amelia. She had no idea what time it was, but she knew it was a new day. A new day to experience, a new day to work, and a new day to begin to live her life anew. The district attorney and assistant district attorney had given her hope.

It was now 2 years later, and she was slowly coming out of her shell of fear. She could think back now without it affecting her. But every now and then, sadness and loneliness came back to haunt her. She was hopeful that one day these feelings would go away.

The timer on the stove was going off, when Amelia realized the cooking timer was trying to get her attention. It let her know that the soup was ready. She shook her head trying to rid herself of the horrific memory, stood up, and walked to the stove. The smell of the soup overriding the memory of what she had been through.

Amelia grabbed her favorite bowl off the shelf and spooned out the vegetable soup into it. Then she walked over to her favorite chair and sat down to watch television and eat.

After her second helping, she put the bowl on the table. Picking up the tv remote, she sneezed and automatically reached into her jacket to get a tissue. She did not have one, but her hand grabbed the envelope and pulled it out. She looked at it again, and held onto it as she stood up, walked to the breakfast bar, grabbed the box of tissues, and walked back to her favorite chair. She grabbed a tissue, blew her nose, and disposed of it.

She then took the envelope, flipped it over and opened it. Inside was a piece of folded stationery paper with a rose in the upper right corner. Her eyes read the simple one sentence message,

"You are beautiful! God has granted you true beauty beginning from the inside and showing on the outside. Your heart is pure, for when you love, you will love with all your heart."

Amelia stared at the paper and was filled with fear and trepidation. Who wrote this note? Why had they sent it to her? Were they trying to scare her?

All the negative thoughts from the previous 4 years came to mind. She read it again, trying to recognize the writing, but to no avail. She kept looking at it repeatedly, her heart finally slowing down a little and her mind clearing slightly as the fear began to ease.

She put the note back into the envelope, stood up, and went to throw it away. But something within her told her not to dispose of it. She walked into the bedroom, took out her favorite wooden box that her dad had made for her, and started to put the envelope inside, when she noticed a scent coming from the envelope. She had no idea what the scent was, but it was pleasant. She finally put the letter in the box, closed it and put it under the bed. Then she walked back to her favorite chair, and tried to resume watching television, but thoughts and questions continued to churn.

CHAPTER 2

It had been a long week, and it was finally Friday. Amelia was looking forward to the weekend. She had hoped to go to the bookstore, then do a little shopping on Saturday; then attend church on Sunday. It had been a long time since she had been able to do exactly what she wanted.

But first, work! Meetings, phones ringing, and constant interruptions…that was her Friday. When she finally locked the door to the insurance office at 5pm, she was relieved. She turned the computers off and locked up her receipt box in the safe. She picked up her purse and keys from her desk, exited and locked the office door. She then walked to her car, entered, and started it. Then she drove out of the parking lot breathing a sigh of relief as she turned onto Dorchester Avenue and headed towards North Charleston and her house.

When she got home, she walked to her mailbox and got the mail out. She looked through it and sorted the junk mail from the bills. She laughed a little as the junk far outnumbered the bills.

Waving at Mrs. Bryant, as she looked out her front window, she was reminded of the women's frailty. She made up her mind to take Mrs. Bryant the leftover vegetable soup that was in the freezer. She walked into the house, opened the freezer, took out the soup in one of the plastic containers. Then she started for the front door.

It had just started to get dark, as she knocked on Mrs. Bryant's door. Mrs. Bryant opened the door with a smile on her face, knowing it was Amelia.

"Amelia, it's so good to see you. How was your day?" Mrs. Bryant said, as Amelia stepped inside. After closing the door, Mrs. Bryant followed Amelia to the kitchen.

"Mrs. Bryant, I made some homemade vegetable soup, thought you might want some," Amelia said, as she put the plastic container into the refrigerator, then turned to see Mrs. Bryant pouring tea into two cups. This was what she did every time Amelia visited. It was something they shared…love of tea.

"Oh, thank you Amelia, you are so sweet," she said, beaming at Amelia. Then Mrs. Bryant handed Amelia a teacup.

After her first sip of tea, curiously, Amelia asked Mrs. Bryant, "Mrs. Bryant, have you ever gotten an anonymous letter in the mail?"

After Mrs. Bryant answered no, Amelia told her about the red envelope and its contents. Mrs. Bryant chuckled, and said, "hmmm, you must have an admirer." Then she sipped her tea, as Amelia thought about what the old lady said.

"I doubt that. I haven't gone out with anyone in so many years. And I have a feeling it will be another few years before I allow myself to date. I've learned my lesson well," Amelia said, remembering what she had gone through.

Amelia and Mrs. Bryant talked about other things. Then she finished her tea and bid Mrs. Bryant good night and left to go home. As she walked back to her house, her mind kept going back to the envelope and letter.

The next morning, Saturday, Amelia slept in, and didn't get up until noon. She jumped into the shower, got dressed, and hurriedly left.

She was on a mission today. First, she would go to the bookstore to grab a couple new releases she had been waiting on, while she drank a cup of coffee. Then, she would head for the mall to see what kind of specials she could get at a bargain price.

After 2 hours, Amelia finally decided to head home. She parked her car in the carport, then walked to the mailbox, and pulled out the mail. Among the junk mail, she saw it. A red envelope with the distinctive rose stamp affixed. Immediately, she felt trepidation, but also a little surprise and intrigue.

Her curiosity forced her to open it while standing at the mailbox. She unfolded the familiar stationery paper with the red rose in the corner, and read the single sentence written on it,

"God made you the way you are. Perfect in every way. Pure heart, clear mind, intelligent, and faith filled."

Amelia didn't know what to make of it. The previous Sunday at church, the pastor had talked about how every human being was made as God had intended. It just seemed odd to her that the sentence in the letter mentioned the same message.

She started thinking back to remember who had been in the church during his sermon, and she could think of no one that might have written the letter. Her mind trying to remember everyone, and every word. She remembered Mr. and Mrs. Anderson, Mr. and Mrs. Castaneda, Mr. and Mrs. Jones being there along with other people she recognized, and few she did not know. As she walked back into the house, she stopped at the open door, turned around and looked around at her neighbors' houses. Her mind kept trying to solve the mystery of who had written the letters.

She closed and locked the front door, then walked to her bedroom. She reached down and picked up the wooden box and opened the lid. The first red envelope stared at her, as if to say, 'yes that other red envelope is my brethren.' Again, she got a hint of a scent on the envelope. The same as the first. She had no idea what it was, but it was intriguing.

Amelia stared at the writing on both the pieces of paper and on the envelope, and it was the same. She noticed that they had been written by what she thought was a fountain pen. "Who uses a fountain pen anymore?" she asked aloud.

She put both letters back into the box, put the box under her bed, and began to change clothes. The entire time she thought about the red envelopes and the letters.

Amelia made herself a sandwich in the kitchen, grabbed a soda, and headed for her favorite chair. Turning on the television and searching for something to watch, her mind kept trying to figure out who had written the letters.

She decided to read instead, and her mind slowly relaxed. She eventually got sleepy, yawned, and turned in for the night. As she began to dream, Amelia's mind remembered her first year in college. How she had struggled through her classes. How she had found it hard to make friends. She dreamed of Lisa, how she had held her, kissed her, and made love to her. She remembered how her Dad had kicked her out of the house, when he had found out she was having an affair with a woman. Her mind remembering the turmoil of her mind as she struggled to fit into her perceived role in society, in family, and in community. They had all shunned her, so she had run away. Charleston was where she found a real home and had met Mark.

She had found a part-time job working in an insurance office. After a year, she had taken and passed the insurance agent state test. The company then had hired her full-time, and she had flourished. Slowly, while dating Mark, her life had become normal. Mark doted on her, and within a year they were married.

Then she remembered how he had changed over their 2 years of marriage, and she awoke from her nightmare sweating and anxious, and breathing hard. She lay back down, and was able to go back to sleep, but her mind was in constant turmoil.

Sunday, she awakened earlier than usual, showered, got dressed, and fixed herself a cup of coffee before she headed for church. When she arrived, she purposely stayed in the vestibule until the last minute, watching people coming in, hoping to solve the mystery. But she couldn't connect anyone she saw to the letters.

Throughout the church service, her mind kept thinking about the letters, so she heard little that the pastor had talked about. She took a moment to look around when the basket was passed around.

Leaving church, she waited in her car until everyone had driven away, as she tried to see if she had missed anyone from earlier. Again, nothing! She just couldn't believe that someone she didn't know had written those letters.

On her way home, Amelia stopped at the Dorchester Diner, and picked up two lunches, one for herself and one for Mrs. Bryant. Then she drove home, took Mrs. Bryant her lunch, and returned to her house.

After changing clothes, she turned the television on and watched one of her favorite shows, as she ate her lunch. But the show held no appeal as her mind kept thinking about the letters. The rest of the afternoon, as she tried to read or watch television, and then went for a walk, all she could think about was, 'who wrote the letters?'

CHAPTER 3

Amelia's ordeal was not over, as the court case against her former husband was coming to trial on Monday. She had met with District Attorney Ashton Mitchell, and Assistant District Attorney Melissa Garner weeks ago. Both had been so protective of her, determined to put her ex-husband away for life.

They discussed her testimony, practicing time and time again, to prepare her for the onslaught of questions she would have to face. She kept her voice steady, showing emotion as she recounted what had happened. The DA's tried to prepare her by saying that Mark's attorney would try to paint her as the instigator. But the DA's had already told her the evidence was solid, and they had very few qualms that he would be found guilty.

The more she thought about the case, the more she resolved not to break on the stand. Resolute to tell her story, to show the jury and everyone that she was the one that had been controlled by him and had suffered at his hand.

Monday seemed to come too quickly. She got up early, had breakfast, dressed, and headed to court. The Assistant District Attorney Melissa Garner met her at the courthouse doors, escorting her to the conference room next door to the courtroom they would be in.

"Amelia, how are you doing this morning?" Melissa asked, concern on her face and in the tone of her voice. Looking at Amelia, Melissa saw the torment on Amelia's face, but she also noticed a glint in her eye. She understood it to be a glint of strength, knowing that Amelia had been so strong for so long. She hoped today would be a good day for Amelia, and not torture. She had been through so much she did not want Amelia to suffer any more. Melissa had noticed that every time she met with Amelia, her smile became more and more relaxed. She was glad that Amelia was slowly starting to come out of her shell.

"I'm good," Amelia said, with strength in her voice. She looked at Melissa, and saw concern, but also saw something she did not recognize. She felt comfortable around Melissa, Amelia thought she wouldn't know what to do if it weren't for Ashton and Melissa.

"Look, you've prepared for this day for a long time. We've gone over everything so many times, we know you've got this. So don't be nervous, and if you do, just look at us. We'll be sitting at the big table in front of you. Just look at me, if it will help you stay calm," Melissa said, hoping her words were helping Amelia.

On the inside, Melissa was concerned for Amelia, but it never showed on her face, demeanor, or body language. She was a professional, trying to help Amelia get through this ordeal.

"Okay. Let's walk into court together. Ashton is already in the court, watching the other side and keeping an eye on everything," Melissa said in a calm voice. As Amelia stood up and headed for the door, Melissa touched her shoulder in reassurance.

They entered the courtroom, and Ashton turned around and smiled at Amelia. Melissa showed Amelia where to sit, directly behind them in the first row of seats.

Amelia sat, and took deep breaths, calming her nerves. Then the marshals brought Mark into the courtroom in handcuffs. They sat him down at the defense table and removed his handcuffs. Immediately, he turned and began to stare at her with an evil grin. She did not respond to his stare and focused on Melissa and Ashton in front of her.

Amelia was calm on the inside, though she thought she would be nervous and jittery. She knew she would get through today. Soon her nightmare would be over.

The bailiff announced the judge, as the judge entered the courtroom and sat in his chair in front of everyone. The judge addressed each attorney, asking for names, so that the Court Reporter could record them into the official record. Then the clerk read aloud the information so it could also be entered into the official record.

Then the judge asked for the jury to enter. All twelve jurors and two alternates entered and took their seats in the jury box. Amelia looked at the faces, one by one, to see if she saw anything that could give her hope. But she knew it was too soon for that and continued staring at Ashton and Melissa to keep herself calm.

After motions, the judge asked for opening arguments. The DA went first and explained what the evidence would prove. The jurors watched him intently, as Amelia watched them. She saw little emotion, which concerned her, but she stayed calm.

After Ashton finished, Mark's attorney stood up and walked toward the jury. He began telling a story that made Mark look like an Angel, and Amelia look like the Devil. Melissa had already discussed this strategy with Amelia, so she was not surprised. She knew every word he said was a lie, but that was his job, to try to keep Mark from going to prison.

Amelia jumped when Mark's attorney pointed at her and spoke her name loudly, saying, "Amelia Thomson started this fight, she is the one that punched Mark first. He was defending himself from her and her onslaught of violence."

Amelia's face blushed, but it was from anger and not embarrassment. She knew the truth, she knew what she would say, she hoped it was enough to send Mark away for an exceedingly long time.

As his attorney finished his opening statements, Mark turned toward her again and gave her an evil grin. Amelia hoped the jury was noticing his behavior, so they could begin to see him the way he really was.

The judge then ordered the DA to begin with witnesses. Ashton called each EMT to the stand, to give their account of what they had seen. The DA put pictures up of the handprint on Amelia's neck. The EMT's had seen them, and acknowledged how severe they were, and her unconscious state when they arrived.

Then the DA called the two police officers that had arrived just before the ambulance, to the stand. Each one told what they had come upon. They had taken statements from Mrs. Bryant, and later from Amelia. Those statements were passed out to the jurors by the DA.

Then the two detectives talked about what their investigation had found. They described the assault in detail, then talked about the evidence. The evidence that proved the assault. Then they discussed Mark's arrest.

Even though Mark's attorney tried to refute the evidence, it was clear that the jury believed what they saw in the pictures and heard from the witnesses.

As each witness came forward and told their stories, it was obvious Mark did not like what they were saying. His expression turned more and more evil as the day progressed. It was also obvious that the jurors were watching his reactions too.

It was nearing 4pm, and the judge decided to call it a day.

Amelia had hoped to get to her testimony today, but it was going to have to wait until tomorrow. Her heart and mind were reeling at the thought of having to think about what she would say the next day…all night long.

Melissa Garner, the ADA, walked Amelia out of the courthouse to her car.

"Amelia, I know you wanted to get your testimony in today, but it was running late. Tomorrow will be all about you and Mrs. Bryant. I want you to go home, have dinner, rest, and be relaxed and prepared for tomorrow," Melissa said, looking at Amelia, seeing the anxiety on her face and concern too. She gave Amelia a hug, and Amelia responded, hugging Melissa back. The hug was comforting and caring.

"Melissa, I promise I'm okay. I wanted it over today too. But tomorrow I can take my time answering questions, and make sure the jury sees what kind of man Mark really is." Amelia said with conviction in her voice. She appreciated Melissa's hug trying to comfort her.

Melissa was awestruck at the resolute tone in Amelia's voice, her demeanor, and her sheer strength of character. She had never had a witness like this in the 4 years as ADA. She continued to look at Amelia with admiration.

"That sounds like you have everything under control Amelia, I'm so glad for you. I promise a few more days and this will be all over. Just hang in there, stay strong…I promise everything will be all right," Melissa said to Amelia, believing in her more now than ever.

Melissa noticed how Amelia's dimples became pronounced when she tried to smile. This woman's suffering made Melissa sick to her stomach. The fact that this woman had survived and begun to thrive proved to Melissa that Amelia was made from the right stuff.

As they parted, they both said goodbye. Melissa watched Amelia head for her car, enter it, turn it on, then saw Amelia wave at her as she drove off.

Amelia was so impressed by Melissa's fortitude, professionalism, and caring nature. She couldn't believe how Melissa could be so caring towards someone she barely knew. Amelia's thoughts changed to concentration as she drove into heavy Charleson traffic.

Amelia made it home safely, parked her car, went to the mailbox, and there was another red envelope. Odd, she had received one last Wednesday, then Saturday. Today was Monday, she did not expect one today. She pulled the envelope from the mailbox and sniffed the envelope and there was that scent again. She held onto it, as she began her walk to her front door. She saw Mrs. Bryant waving at her through her front window. She waved and smiled back to her…it was always good to know Mrs. Bryant had her eyes peeled on everything that went on in the neighborhood.

Entering her house, Amelia closed and locked the front door, then took her jacket off. She continued to hold the red envelope as she trekked to the kitchen to start her tea kettle. After starting it, she gathered her favorite teacup and spoon. Then she sat down at the kitchen table.

While waiting for the tea kettle to finish, she opened the red envelope, unfolded the rose stationery, and read the handwriting,

"Inner strength and courage are yours when life becomes difficult. Let your faith, friends, and special ones give you their guidance so you can find what you are looking for."

She thought of what had happened to her at the hands of Mark, how she had survived and then begun to flourish. She thought about the court case, and her testimony that was expected the next day. She knew it would take all her inner strength to stay calm, cool, and collected tomorrow. She thought about all the women she helped at work as an insurance agent, and the strength and courage they had to have to protect their families.

Over the last couple of months, she had begun to explore the possibility of becoming a social worker, so she could help other women that were going through the same things she had gone through. She felt like she needed to be able to help others so she could finish healing.

Putting the letter back in the envelope, she smelled the scent again and the word 'Lavender' popped into her head. She was sure that the scent was lavender. She had smelled that before, but she couldn't place it.

She was tired from today, and as she finished her tea, she yawned. Looking at the clock, she realized she had been sitting at the table for over an hour. She rinsed her cup out, put it in the dish rack, along with her spoon, and walked into her bedroom.

She took the wooden box out from beneath her bed and put the red envelope in it with the others. As she put the box back under the bed, her thoughts went to the question, 'who had written them?'

A minute later she changed out of her court clothes and put her sweatpants and sweatshirt on. Then added warm socks. The night was going to be cool, so she wanted to stay warm.

She grabbed one of the new books she had bought Saturday and nestled down into her comfortable mattress surrounded by soft pillows. She started reading the book, but it wasn't long before she nodded off.

Amelia dreamed that night, but she was disturbed by her dream. She had dreamed that a faceless woman had made love to her during the night.

When she had awakened, she said aloud, "Where the hell had that come from?" She thought about her dream. She believed she was straight, since she had dated men. But she remembered Lisa and her college days. Her dream made her realize that no man had ever made her feel like she felt right now. The woman was faceless, but her hands and body had made Amelia feel things she had never felt before.

Geez! Was she going insane? What was happening to her? She just could not fathom where that dream had come from. It really disturbed her, but it excited her at the same time.

Realizing she was not going to be able to go back to sleep, Amelia decided to get up and take a hot shower. That might settle her nerves.

She took her time since she had awakened so early. She made herself breakfast and had two cups of coffee. She checked her emails and made notes that she texted to her business partner, Sandra. Then she washed up, brushed her teeth, and blow dried her hair. Then, she took her time applying her makeup.

She went through her wardrobe and picked out her favorite navy pants with a matching double-breasted blazer and added a white mock neck. She found her favorite pumps she liked to wear with her suit too.

She accessorized it with gold hoop earrings, a gold bangle bracelet, and a simple cross her parents had given her for her 13th birthday. She grabbed a navy clutch she really liked and that looked good with what she was wearing.

Looking in the mirror, she looked like she was prepared for anything and everything. She knew today was the day she could tell her story and effectively change her life forever. She thought, 'why am I taking such great care to look good?' 'What is going on with me?' Questions for which she had no answers, yet!

She looked at the time, and realized it was time for her to leave the house. She walked out, locked up, and went to her car. She started it, then backed out. Her trip to the courthouse took about 15 minutes. She found a parking spot and started to walk towards the courthouse.

Then Amelia heard, "Amelia, wait up." She turned to see Melissa Garner, the assistant DA walking towards her.

"How are you doing this morning?" Melissa said, as she smiled at Amelia.

"Good. I am ready for today. I just want to get it over with, and get my new life started," Amelia said with a positive tone in her voice, as she smiled at Melissa.

"Today is the day your new life begins, and your old life ends. I'm glad I am here to see it," Melissa said, her tone a little emotional.

"Thank you, Melissa. You and Ashton have been so supportive, I don't know how I'll ever repay you," Amelia said sincerely.

"Just live your life to the fullest. You have the inner strength and courage to do or be anything you want. You achieving your best is payment enough," Melissa said, as they climbed the stairs to the doors at the front of the courthouse.

Amelia's mind went to the letter that had mentioned inner strength and courage, and it seemed odd that Melissa would mention the same thing today. But, as they entered the courthouse, Amelia forgot the coincidence.

Walking toward the courtroom, Melissa excused herself as she left to go into the Clerk-of-Court's office. Amelia continued to the courtroom, getting slightly nervous as she approached the doors to enter. As she did, Ashton Mitchell, the DA, saw her and said, "Amelia, you ready?"

"Hi Ashton. I'm a little nervous, but I want to get this over with so I can start anew," Amelia said, remembering the conversation she just had with Melissa.

"Well, you are the second witness today, after Mrs. Bryant. I just talked to her, and she is ready to tell her story. Then closing arguments, and then jury instructions. So, we may still be here for a couple of hours. But I promise you, there is nothing his attorney could say that can change the damning evidence from yesterday. I'll remind the jury about that during closing arguments. They will understand what happened and will find Mark guilty. I don't want you to worry, okay?" Ashton said in a confident tone, trying to reassure Amelia.

"Okay. Thank you, Ashton. I can't thank you and Melissa enough." Amelia said earnestly.

Sitting down, Amelia took the same seat as yesterday. Then she noticed Melissa walk into the court from another door and sit at the big table in front of her next to Ashton. She noticed Melissa leaning toward Ashton to say something in a low tone she could not hear. She also noticed that Melissa took out a fountain pen and wrote something down. Odd she thought, 'I thought fountain pens were out of style.' Quickly, her mind returned to today's proceedings as she noticed the left side door open.

Marshals brought Mark into the packed courtroom, sat him

at the defense table, and released him from his handcuffs. Then the bailiff announced the judge as he walked into the courtroom and took his seat, like yesterday. After the clerk of the court made several announcements. Then the jury was brought in and took their seats. The judge asked the DA to continue to his next witness.

The DA called Mrs. Bryant to the stand. He asked her to describe what had happened on that fateful day. She described the blood-curdling scream and shouting she had heard. She also described her conversation with the 911 operator. Her face showed great emotion recalling those events in detail.

After the DA had finished with Mrs. Bryant, then the defense asked her questions. It was obvious he was trying to trip up Mrs. Bryant. But she still had a sharp mind, stayed calm, and used very descriptive language when asked about Mark, Amelia, and the events of that day.

It was obvious the testimony had the jury's attention, as they kept looking between Mrs. Bryant and Mark. Amelia watched the jury closely, looking for any signs on their faces. But they were concentrating on Mrs. Bryant's testimony, were showing no emotions.

As the defense attorney finished with Mrs. Bryant, Mark turned in his chair again, stared and grinned at Amelia. Amelia saw him out of the corner of her eye and continued to stare at Melissa and Ashton sitting in front of her. She would not allow Mark to intimidate her no matter what.

Next, the DA called her name, she stood up and walked toward the witness box. The bailiff swore her in, and the DA started his questioning.

"Amelia, please tell us about that fateful day when your ex-husband attacked you and you ended up in the hospital," Ashton said, looking directly at Amelia and smiling slightly to make her feel comfortable in the witness box. Then he moved to block Mark's vantage point.

"I came home from work around 530pm. I had forgotten to stop by the grocery store, so when I walked in, Mark asked me about dinner. I told him that I had forgotten to stop to pick up the groceries and would cook something else. He began yelling at me, that he "wanted what he wanted," and that I "was stupid for forgetting," and that I "was good for nothing."

"Then his face started to turn really red. His breathing became heavy and loud. He rushed toward where I stood in the living room. I tried to turn and run out the door, but he grabbed me by the neck. I screamed as loud as I could. I tried to fight him off, but he was just too powerful. He continued choking me until I passed out." Amelia recounted her story calmly, as if it was someone else's story. But she knew the hard part was coming up after the DA finished his questions.

"What happened when you woke up?" The DA asked, again looking at Amelia with concern.

"I came to in the ambulance, and they administered oxygen. At the hospital I was examined by the doctors in the emergency room. Dr. Albertson told me that I was incredibly lucky. He told me I came within seconds of death. He ordered lab tests, and breathing treatments every 4 hours, to keep my swollen neck from interrupting my breathing. I was ordered to rest. I spent two days in the hospital until all the tests came back and the swelling in my neck had gone down." Amelia again, calm, and resolute as she told her story to the jury.

"Is this the only time Mark had put his hands on you in

anger?" The DA had prepared Amelia for this question.

Amelia took a deep breath and began, "that was the only time he choked me out. But he had been sexually aggressive with me quite a few times, and I had told him he hurt me. But he wouldn't stop. Then there were the times he slapped me too."

"How quickly after you married did his personality change?" the DA asked, hoping to convince the jury that Mark was a menace from early on.

"His personality seemed to change within just a month or so after we married. It's like he was another person suddenly," Amelia said, recalling the beginning of her ordeal.

"What was his demeanor like normally?" the DA asked, wanting to set a precedence of Mark's behavior.

Amelia took a deep breath, and said, "He was controlling. He always told me what to wear. We never went out to eat, he always wanted me home as soon after work as possible. He never let me go out shopping except to the grocery store. If we needed something else, he would drive and go in with me wherever we went. I had to ask him for money, even though I made more money than he did. It's like he just couldn't let me be me," Amelia finished looking down at her hands, realizing they were clammy.

"Thank you, Amelia. I'm finished your honor," the DA said, walking to his chair and sitting down.

"The defense may now question the witness," the judge said, as the defense attorney got up and started walking toward Amelia.

"Ms. Thomson, when you dated Mark, did he ever touch you in a bad way?" the defense attorney asked.

"No, when we dated, he seemed to be loving and caring," Amelia said.

"I see. So, Mark didn't change until after he married you, is that correct?" he asked Amelia. Amelia started to answer the question when he asked another.

"Weren't you the cause of that change Amelia? Isn't it true that you withheld sex from Mark to spite him working late?" the defense attorney posited.

Immediately Amelia answered, "absolutely not. He became sexually aggressive within weeks of our marriage. I complained to him that he was hurting me, and to please stop. But it just got worse."

"Is it true, that you would deliberately stay at work later, so Mark had to do the cooking?" the attorney asked her.

Amelia answered, "there were times I had to work late. I didn't expect him to get mad about that. He is the one that insisted I cook all the meals, since he was "King" of his own home."

"So, you expect us to believe that Mark just changed out of the blue, became sexually aggressive towards you, yelled at you, choked you out for no reason? Is that right?" the defense attorney asked, waiting for Amelia to answer.

"I did not do anything to Mark. I worked hard during the day, went home and cooked and cleaned. Then he expected rough sex every night. He wouldn't give me any money, though I made more than he did. He controlled me from day one," Amelia said, her mind filling with all the times he had forced her into sex, yelled at her, and made her feel like she was worthless.

"Well Amelia, I don't believe you. But thank you for your answer," said the defense attorney, as he returned to his seat. "No further questions your honor," the defense had finished questioning Amelia.

"Objection your honor. Improper utterance," Ashton stood up and loudly proclaimed to the judge.

The judge, looking disdainfully at the defense attorney, then looked at the jury and said, "that last statement will be stricken from the record as improper. The jury is to invalidate what the defense attorney has uttered." Again, he looked at the defense attorney and gave him an admonishing look.

The defense had finished questioning Amelia. She stepped down and looked toward Ashton and Melissa as she returned to her seat behind them. She did not look at Mark, she just did not want to see his evil looks.

The judge then asked the DA if he had any further witnesses, to which Ashton replied "no, your Honor. We have no further witnesses." The judge then announced they would take a 30-minute break, then return for closing arguments, and jury instructions.

Amelia was relieved that her part was over. Melissa and Ashton walked Amelia to the conference room next to the courtroom, and ushered her in.

They chatted about what would happen next and told Amelia that she did not have to be there again until sentencing. But Amelia wanted to be there until the very end. They urged her to go home, and that they would call her when the verdict came in from the jury.

Melissa understood it would be cathartic for Amelia to see this through to the end. Ashton understood too and agreed. Amelia finally acquiesced and left to go home. Ashton and Melissa watched her walk off.

They returned to court after the allotted time, and the DA was instructed to give his closing arguments. He reminded the jurors of the evidence they had seen, and that it had been corroborated by the EMT's and police that had arrived on the scene quickly. Then he reminded them of the investigators' reports that showed how Mark had committed the atrocity against Amelia. He also reminded them of their duty to review the evidence, not just the statements.

Then he closed his arguments with, "you have seen the evidence, you have heard the witnesses, you have seen the witnesses testify. You are intelligent enough to know that the consistencies in statements and evidence proves without a shadow of a doubt that Mark Thomson tried to murder Amelia Thomson. You must find him guilty. Make him pay for what he did to Amelia. Lock him up so he won't try this on anyone else in the future."

When Ashton finished speaking, there was total silence in the courtroom. But Mark's evil look had deepened. It was obvious to anyone that looked at him, just as Amelia had done when Ashton finished his closing arguments.

Then it was the defense attorney's turn. He posited that it was Amelia that was the aggressor, and that it was she who had instigated the argument. And, that she was the one that had turned violent when Mark had asked her about the grocery items. Mark had just tried to defend himself from the violent onslaught brought on by Amelia. When he finished his closing argument he walked and sat down in his chair.

Melissa tried not to read anything into the fact that jurors looked at Mark, then at the judge.

The judge then began to give his instructions to the jury. They had a choice, they could find Mark not guilty, guilty of first-degree assault, or guilty of attempted murder. He explained the difference between first degree assault and attempted murder.

He asked them to consider the evidence closely, as well as the witness statements. He also informed them that they would deliberate and cast votes until the vote was unanimous, or they would have to declare a mistrial. He excused the jury so they could go to the deliberation room.

The judge then declared the court in recess until the jury returned with a verdict. Everyone stood up while the judge walked out, the marshals handcuffed Mark and took him out of the courtroom, and the court officials left. It was 1130am when the jury started. No one knew how long it would take to return the verdict.

Melissa exhaled from relief and exhaustion. She and Ashton turned around and began to leave the courtroom.

"I think that went well," Ashton was the first one to speak, trying to reassure Melissa. It was obvious she was feeling the stress of the trial.

"I agree, I think the jury understood what happened," Melissa said, thinking of Amelia. She remembered Amelia's dark eyes, and the look on her face during the trial. It was hard to forget.

At 3pm of the same day, the jury sent a message to the judge that they had finished deliberating and had reached a verdict. Ashton and Melissa received the message from the bailiff via text message and called Amelia to come back to the courtroom. 20 minutes later, Amelia arrived. They saw the anxiety on her face and tried to reassure her with a smile.

The three of them returned to the same courtroom. Shortly thereafter, the marshals brought Mark back into the courtroom and removed his handcuffs. The judge then entered, and so did the jury.

The judge asked the jury if they had reached a unanimous verdict, and the foreperson said, "Yes." The court clerk walked to the foreperson and retrieved the envelope, opened it, and handed it to the judge. The judge then asked the foreperson to read the verdict.

"We, the jury, in the case of the State of South Carolina versus Mark Thomson, find as to the charge of first-degree assault, innocent. As to the charge of attempted murder, we find the defendant, 'Guilty!'."

The courtroom exploded with emotion. Amelia began crying, and Melissa and Ashton tried to console her. Mark began shouting that he was "innocent" and starting pounding the table. Quickly the bailiff's got him under control and handcuffed him, then made him sit down. The judge banged his gavel trying to calm the courtroom down.

"Order, order in the court," the judge repeated several times before all the commotion settled.

"Jurors, I would like to thank you for your service and hereby excuse you to leave the courtroom. Clerk, please see them out," the judge instructed. The jury stood up and filed out following the Clerk into the nearby room.

"Attorney's, you have until Thursday noon to file any appeals," the judge said, looking at the defense, whose head hung in defeat.

"I will need the District Attorneys sentencing recommendation by tomorrow noon. I want both sets of attorneys and the defendant back here at 2pm Thursday for sentencing. Is there any further business we need to discuss?" the judge asked, but no one said a thing. He then dismissed the court and exited.

Melissa and Ashton turned to see Amelia crying. Melissa came around and sat next to Amelia, put her arms around her, in a hug, feeling the relief coming from her.

"We did it Amelia. You did it!" Melissa said into Amelia's ear, hoping to comfort Amelia. Amelia was thankful that Melissa was there for her. She was thankful that Ashton and Melissa were so good at their jobs. She cried happy tears.

As the crying eased off, Melissa released Amelia. She wiped tears from Amelia's face and gave her an incredible look. Then the moment was gone. Amelia had no idea what that had been, but it had made her feel alive.

That night, Amelia thought about the day she had experienced, and her mind kept going back to the look that Melissa had given her. She could not fathom what that look had meant.

As she drifted off to sleep, she thought about that look, and for some reason it brought her comfort.

CHAPTER 4

Monday had been so traumatic, but not as much as Tuesday, when she had to take the stand. Amelia was exhausted. She felt like she couldn't do one thing today.

She felt relieved that it was Wednesday. It was early, 6am, when she woke up, but she called her business partner, Sandra, and told her she would not be in today. She explained she was exhausted. Sandra understood what Amelia had just experienced and agreed with her.

Amelia went back to bed and fell asleep. Awakened by a dream hours later, it was that same dream again. A faceless woman that made love to her. This time the desire seemed real. Her body was still responding to the mental stimuli.

'How is this possible?'... 'Why am I having this dream?'... 'Why is my body responding like this?' Amelia asked herself. But no answers came.

She lay in bed thinking about her dream, but the more she thought about it, the more her body responded. She decided to stop its impending conclusion.

To try to calm her body down, Amelia grabbed her phone from the side of the bed and looked to see the time. Then she looked to see if she had any messages. Nothing urgent or out of the ordinary she thought. She got up and headed for the shower, hoping to qualm the desire that had made itself known in her dream.

The hot shower cascaded over her body, and she drowned her head in its caress. She then grabbed the fragrant soap she loved to indulged in and began to lather. She recognized the scent as lavender. Again, that scent that she couldn't get out of her mind. She realized that thinking of that scent brought warmth to her, not what she had expected.

She turned the shower to a colder setting, sending chills through her body as she rinsed the soap off. The effect was immediate, no desire could live through that freezing water.

After showering, Amelia dressed in jeans and her favorite sweatshirt and added socks and her favorite walking sneakers. She blow-dried her hair and left it loose, cascading over her shoulders and down her back.

Looking at herself in the mirror, she realized she looked different today. She looked relaxed, rested, and more herself than in quite a while. She was glad that the shell of fear was finally breaking.

She walked down the hallway and into the kitchen, tapping the coffee maker to start, since she had prepared it the previous evening.

She opened the fridge and grabbed four eggs, put them into a pot of water and boiled them on the stove. Knowing it would take about 20 minutes to finish, she walked into the living room. Drawing back the drapes on the big living room window, she noticed the mail carrier opening her mailbox, putting the letters into it, and closing it before he drove off.

Amelia opened the front door, bracing herself for the cold that came rushing in. She quickly walked to the mailbox, grabbed the mail from within, and walked back briskly to get out of the cold.

Returning inside, she closed and locked the front door. She then headed back into the kitchen to sit at the kitchen table to sort through the mail. Junk mail greeted her, but she noticed the corner of the red envelope sticking out of a large multi-paged marketing piece from a local furniture store. She quickly separated it from the rest of the mail, her mind and body a little excited to see what it held.

Amelia opened it slowly, withdrew the familiar stationery with the red rose in the upper right-hand corner and read it, **"Life begins, love begins, dreams begin."**

Again, the same handwriting. Again, the same scent.

Now, the letter brought back to life the dream she had during the night. She just couldn't get the sensualness of the note and the dream out of her head. She shook her head, not understanding how she could feel this way.

The timer on the stove went off and Amelia busied herself rinsing and peeling the eggs. She then made toast to which she added her favorite guacamole and fixed herself a cup of coffee. Sitting at the kitchen table, she continued to daydream about the red envelopes, the letters within, and her dream. Her body quickly responded.

Wanting to quell the rising desire, Amelia decided to do household chores. She vacuumed, then cleaned the bathroom. She tossed a load of dirty clothes into the washer. Then she decided she was going to read until the washing machine signaled it was done.

Nestled down into her favorite reading chair, she nodded off. The brief time she was in the chair, the dream reappeared. Her body responded accordingly, and again, she awakened in the middle of the arousal.

Wow, wow, wow! She thought as she tried to control her body. Amelia realized she had to get away from the dream. She got up, went into the bathroom, and freshened up. She decided she was going to go for a drive. The day had finally turned nice, after starting out gray and cold. The sun had come out and was being teased by puffy clouds that skirted through the sky.

She picked up a fleeced jacket from the chair where she had left it, grabbed her keys and wallet, and exited her house. After getting into the car, starting it, she decided to drive to Sullivans Island, her favorite beach.

25 minutes later, Amelia found a public parking space, paid for the parking stub, and walked through the public access to her favorite stretch of beach.

The sun was strong, but the wind was cool, and blustery. She was thrilled that there were very few people out and about. She started walking towards the inlet, her mind full of thoughts from the last few weeks.

Amelia found herself walking briskly to keep herself warm, and it made her feel energized. Before she knew it, she had reached the inlet and sat down in the sand to catch her breath. She looked out into the ocean and noticed the large container ships headed toward the shipping docks on the Port of Charleston.

She noticed the pelicans flying in the traditional follow the leader formation. She saw the sandlappers and seagulls on the shore looking for tidbits to consume. The dolphins jumping in the water of the inlet made her smile. Her mind quickly cleared itself of the traumatic happenings, and of her dreams that had brought unusual feelings to the surface.

After 20 minutes or so Amelia decided to walk back to where she had started. She was daydreaming when she heard her name being called. "Amelia is that you?" a familiar voice said. As Amelia turned, she noticed it was Melissa from the DA's office. She was dressed in dark sweats, a grey fleece jacket, and a baseball cap with a Clemson paw on it.

"Hi Melissa, what are you doing out here?" Amelia asked, a little surprised to see her on a workday. Melissa's face lit up with a smile, and Amelia returned it.

"I decided to take a day off. I've been working so hard lately, Ashton suggested I take it off," Melissa said, standing next to Amelia.

"Oh, that's good. I took today off too. I just needed to unwind from the last 2 days," Amelia said, remembering the exhaustion she had felt this morning. But, as she was talking, she realized that now she felt even more energized.

"Can I walk with you? Of course, if you don't want me to, that's okay, I would understand," Melissa said, looking hopeful at Amelia.

Amelia quickly responded without thinking, "Melissa, I would enjoy us walking together. Come on, let's head for the lighthouse," Amelia said smiling, as she turned and started walking briskly toward the lighthouse. Melissa picked up her pace and was soon walking next to Amelia.

"How are you feeling today?" Melissa asked, concern for Amelia noticeable.

"I'm fine. I woke up exhausted this morning. I didn't sleep well last night either, a dream woke me up," Amelia said without thinking. Her mind going back to the desire filled dream she'd had.

"What was the dream about?" Melissa asked innocently. Suddenly, Amelia's face turned red and filled with embarrassment.

"I'm not sure I can talk about it," Amelia hesitated, her voice catching a moment, making Melissa look at her.

"Are you okay, was it a nightmare?" Melissa asked, looking with concern at Amelia, her eyes questioning what Amelia had said.

"No, most definitely not a nightmare," Amelia said, with an odd tone in her voice. "I'm not sure I can talk about it. It's like no dream I've ever had before. I'm still trying to figure out why I had it," Amelia tried to skirt Melissa's interest in her dream.

"Oh, I'm sorry. I'm so used to asking questions, sometimes it gets the better of me. I apologize if I made you feel uncomfortable," Melissa said in an apologetic tone.

To Amelia, it was clear that Melissa had asked her out of concern, and not to pry. "That's okay. This is the second time I've had this same dream, and I can't figure out why," Amelia said, trying to explain without going into details.

"Sometimes our dreams don't mean anything. They can be triggered by anything on our minds, things happening, or even a scent or particular words. When I was in college, I dreamed that a red car appeared every time I thought about going out on a date with a man. It wasn't until 6 months later that I realized I was a lesbian," Melissa admitted, not looking at Amelia.

Amelia responded, "I would never have guessed that." The look on her face showing surprise. "I'm sorry if that came out awkward. I'm sure it was extremely hard for you."

"That's okay Amelia. Yes, it was at first. My parents and I fought my entire sophomore year in college. I came close to flunking. But my brother James helped me to see that my parents just didn't know how to react, since their upbringing had been so conservative. I decided to forgive them and throw myself into my classes. So, I finished college, then went on to law school. Ashton recruited me straight out of law school with no experience. That was 4 years ago. My life is my own now." Melissa's voice sounded firm but comforting.

"I'm sorry you had to go through that with your parents. My belief is God made you how and who you are. You don't mess with perfection," Amelia said, remembering the sermon and the letter.

"That's really nice of you to say." Melissa replied, looking at Amelia with a smile on her face.

The wind was really blowing now, and it looked like clouds were starting to come in.

"Looks like the sun is over, and clouds are coming, bringing in a storm. We had better get out of here," Amelia said, looking out over the beach at the ocean and sky.

Melissa had stopped too, but she wasn't looking at the ocean. She was looking at Amelia. The wind was tousling amelia's hair, and it looked like she had a halo. Amelia noticed Melissa's stare, as she looked at Melissa. Melissa quickly looked away, trying to hide her stare.

"I had better get going, I've got a bit to walk to get to my car," Melissa said, looking down at the sand, a little embarrassed that Amelia had caught her staring.

"I'm close by, I can drive you if you want," Amelia said, noticing Melissa's embarrassment.

"That's okay, I really need the exercise. I'll see you Sunday at church," Melissa said, as she started to walk in the opposite direction, not waiting for Amelia's reply.

Amelia noticed Melissa's quick departure, and shouted, "See you Sunday," as Melissa sprinted off. It came to Amelia that she had seen Melissa at church several Sundays in the last year, and it brought her comfort.

Amelia walked to her car, and just as she reached it, a slow drizzle started. She sat there for a minute thinking about her conversation with Melissa. It was sad what Melissa had to endure. Amelia hoped Melissa had found happiness in her life.

She slowly drove home, her thoughts jumping from one thing to another. Getting home, she parked, unlocked the door, and entered the house. As she turned around after locking the door, she saw the red envelope on the table that she had received earlier.

Amelia picked it up, and reread the note inside, **"Life begins, love begins, dreams begin."**

How prophetic Amelia thought. Whoever this person was, they knew her somehow. She just couldn't understand who or how.

CHAPTER 5

The following day, Amelia awakened at her normal time and realized that today was the day they were sentencing Mark. She wanted to be there, though Ashton and Melissa had told her she didn't have to be there.

Amelia was insistent on completing this final chapter of her old life. She wanted to see the look on Mark's face when he was sentenced. She wanted to see the look on his face when they took him away for the final time. She felt like that would bring her closure.

She quickly showered, dressed, and left the house. She stopped by the office to see if Sandra was okay, she felt guilty at leaving her by herself so much since all this mess started. Luckily, this was the slow part of the year in the office.

Sandra saw Amelia park and exit her car. She met Amelia at the door and hugged her as soon as she came through the door. It took Amelia by surprise; she didn't have time to say anything.

"Hi honey, how are you feeling? Are you okay?" Sandra enquired as Amelia looked at Sandra's face and saw the concern.

"Sandra, I'm fine. Please stop all this fussing. I just wanted to check on you before I head to the courthouse for the final time," Amelia said, trying to reassure Sandra she was okay.

"They are sentencing him today, right?" Sandra said, trying to reassure herself this was almost over too.

"Yes. Today is the day. They said the court would reconvene at 2 today, so I have a little time. Thought I would check my emails before heading to the courthouse. This shouldn't take me long at all," Amelia said, as she sat at her desk, touched her computer to life, and waited for it to boot.

"Shouldn't be anything of importance. Most of our clients call if they need anything right away. But I know you love to go through emails every day and get rid of the junk. I don't blame you, I hate that stuff," Sandra chuckled, as she returned to her desk to answer the phone.

Amelia quickly logged in, brought up her business email account, and started to look through her messages. She blocked junk mail as she scrolled, and realized there was nothing she needed. She logged out and turned her computer off.

"You were right Sandra, nothing but junk," Amelia said with a slight chuckle and smiled at Sandra. She checked the mail on the desk, and nothing of importance was there either. She threw the junk mail out and filed the two bills to reconcile at the end of the month.

"All right Sandra, I've got a little time, so I'm going to grab a coffee before heading to the courthouse. I'll call you afterwards and let you know what happened," Amelia said, knowing Sandra would want to know right away.

"You do that, I'll be waiting," Sandra said, smiling and nodding at Amelia as she began to walk out.

Amelia reached her car and headed toward the nearest drive-thru coffee stand. The coffee was better than she remembered, as she sipped it driving to the courthouse. She parked in the courthouse lot, and continued to drink her coffee, passing time until she had to be in court.

At 1:45, she entered the courtroom and sat down in her usual spot. Ashton and Melissa had not arrived yet. But she noticed the court officers and staff in place. As she finished looking around, Ashton and Melissa entered the court and took their place at the DA's table. They turned and smiled at her but had no time to talk to her as the marshals ushered Mark into the courtroom in handcuffs. This time they didn't remove the handcuffs. Mark's body language, with his head hanging down, showed him defeated. His attorney seated next to him, did not look well either.

The bailiff announced the judge as he came in and took his seat as well. The judge began, "Order in the court" he said firmly.

"Attorneys, I have received no appeal paperwork. But I have received your sentencing recommendations. I have reviewed all the evidence, and witness statements. I have also reviewed any precedence that could help the court decide proper punishment for this crime," the judge stopped talking, readjusting in his seat.

"All that being said," he restarted, "Mark Thomson, please rise," the judge ordered. Mark rose slowly, knowing his fate was here.

"Having been found guilty of the charge of Attempted Murder, I hereby sentence you to 25 years, without the possibility of parole. Though this is your first violent offence, I want to send a clear message to any man that decides to do the same to his significant other, that this type of behavior is not tolerated," the judge spoke, and you could see Mark's energy dissipate and his legs begin to shake.

"I further order, that any properties, monies, and personal items be transferred forthwith to Amelia Thomson as compensation for the atrocity which you committed upon her body. This is in fulfilling the recently passed law and legislation Victim's Protection Act. This I so order to occur as per the law within 30 days. Mr. Thomson, what that means is that you hereby forfeit all your worldly possessions and money; they will be transferred to the possession of Amelia Thomson for her benefit and in compensation for the act of attempted murder. Marshals, you may take Mr. Thomson into federal custody. This court is now dismissed," the judge finished.

The entire courtroom could be heard exhaling as the Marshals marched Mark out of the courtroom. Amelia's breath caught in her chest. She still could not believe she was here, what had happened to her, and how her life had changed so quickly. She was free!

Ashton and Melissa turned around and both hugged Amelia at the same time, Ashton saying, "he got his due."

"Amelia, you are free at last," Melissa said, looking at Amelia with an incredible smile on her face.

Amelia nodded in agreement, tears welling up. She felt Ashton and Melissa's arms around her, and it gave her great comfort.

As they walked out of the courthouse, Amelia felt such a relief. Ashton and Melissa kept looking at her, making sure she was okay.

When they reached the bottom steps of the courthouse, Amelia spoke, "Ashton and Melissa, thank you for giving me my life back. I can't thank you enough, both of you."

Ashton spoke first, "Amelia, just go and live your life. Learn to live again, learn to love again, and allow yourself to dream again."

Melissa said smiling at Amelia, "Ashton is right, I love that quote by Margaret Taylor. She went through the same as you did. When her trial was over, she spoke to other women, and that is exactly what she told them. Amelia, we believe you will quickly recover from this."

"Thank you both again. I promise to live my life to the fullest," she said, as she started to walk away. She nodded and waved to both, as she walked to her car.

CHAPTER 6

Amelia sat in her car for a few minutes. Her heart lighter now, her emotions on a positive note. She wanted to celebrate, so she stopped at the bakery on the way to the office, and picked up Sandra's favorite pastry, and coffee. Then she drove to the office.

She pulled into the parking lot in front of the office, when Sandra opened the door and greeted her. Upon seeing the bakery box, Sandra became very animated.

"Amelia, tell me everything that happened in court today. Who was there? What did the judge say? How do you feel?" all the questions she threw at Amelia made Amelia laugh.

"Whoa girl, I can't answer but one question at a time," Amelia said, laughing at Sandra. As they began discussing the day's events, she and Sandra consumed the tasty pastries and coffee.

However, Amelia's mind kept returning to the letters she had been getting. She had not told Sandra about the letters. She felt she wanted to keep it private until she could figure out who had written them.

After consuming the pastries and coffee, Amelia decided to go home. Arriving home, Amelia parked her car, went to the mailbox, and retrieved the mail. More junk mail again, so she waited until she got into the house before sorting it.

She saw it as she was sorting. Another red envelope. She was excited, so she went ahead and opened it, unfolded the stationery, and read what it said,

"Dream of living, dream of loving, nothing is beyond you. You

are free to find your future, define your life, and to explore love. Dream your dreams."

Understanding its message, she was taken aback. How could the writer know she was dreaming? How did they know? She could not answer her own question. She still did not know who was writing the letters, but she had a feeling she already knew them.

Inserting the letter back in the envelope, she walked to the bedroom and added the envelope to the others in the wooden box. She kept a script in her head of what the letters said,

"You are beautiful! God has granted you true beauty beginning from the inside and showing on the outside. Your heart is pure, for when you love, you will love with all your heart."

"God made you the way you are. Perfect in every way. Pure heart, clear mind, intelligent, and faith filled."

"Inner strength and courage are yours when life becomes difficult. Let your faith, friends, and special ones give you their guidance so you can find what you are looking for."

"Life begins, love begins, dreams begin,"

"Dream of living, dream of loving, nothing is beyond you. You are free to find your future, define your life, and to explore love. Dream your dreams."

Like a mantra she repeated the sayings in her head, and her heart began to believe them.

She gasped a ragged breath, and started crying, overwhelmed by the feelings evoked by the letters. Amelia believed that whoever was writing her the letters knew her better than she knew herself. She was looking forward to what the next letters would say, and how they would make her feel.

CHAPTER 7

Over the next few weeks Amelia's life seemed to return to normal. She allowed herself to think about her future.

She visited the local college to see what she would need to get her degree in social work. She learned that all those classes she had taken online over the years were all transferable; so, she had enough credits to only have to do her last 2 years of coursework to get her degree. And the courses she needed were offered at night, so she could still work as an insurance agent during the day.

She visited the women's shelter and began to volunteer. She learned how to answer the bank of phones when women called in and needed help. She did this on alternating Saturday and Sunday nights.

Five red envelopes arrived over those weeks, bringing messages she became intrigued to read.

"Love comes from the heart, listen to your heart. Too often we allow our minds to stop listening, but our hearts know what they want."

"When you least expect it love will find you. Will you be brave enough to recognize it.'

"Living life to its fullest, accepting everyday as it comes, allows love to grow in your heart."

"Don't let preconceived notions about love guide your heart. Your heart is pure, it only knows real love and kindness. Let it feel."

"The face of love may be obscured, but the reality of love is clear. Do not try to hide from it, let it come in."

Every day she looked forward to getting the mail. While at work, she thought about the letters. While at college at night, she thought about the letters. The letters consumed her thoughts night and day.

While on campus of the local college, and while registering for another class, she heard a familiar voice. She turned around to see ADA Melissa Gardner talking with someone. Before she could even see her face, Amelia's heart skipped a beat.

She waited for Melissa to finish talking with what looked like an instructor, before approaching her.

"Melissa is that you?" she asked smiling, already knowing the answer before Melissa turned around.

"Amelia, so good to see you," Melissa smiled back and gave Amelia a hug. Amelia hugged her back like a long-lost friend. "How have you been?" Melissa continued.

"I've been very well, thank you. Working like crazy and I just registered for two classes towards my social work degree. What are you doing here?" Amelia asked, so proud of herself.

Melissa noticed Amelia was doing great. There was light in her eyes, she had gained a little weight that filled her out nicely. Her smile was incredible. Amelia stood taller and prouder. Melissa was excited for her.

"That is great! I'm so glad you are pursuing your dreams. It so good to see you doing well." Melissa said smiling at Amelia. Then she added, "I'm teaching a law class at night, 3 nights a week. Now that I have the time, I thought it would be great to give back to my alma mater."

"I heard Ashton just became Attorney General for the state of South Carolina. Does that mean you're the new District A?" Amelia asked, hoping Melissa had found greater success.

"Actually, shortly after the last time I saw you, I left the DA's office, and now I'm a partner at a law firm. My best friend and I decided to open our own office. It's been a little crazy, but we both love it. We specialize in helping women through divorce, violence intervention, and family law. It is a calling for both of us." Melissa said, showing her pride by offering Amelia her new business card.

"Oh Melissa, I'm so proud of you. That is wonderful. I know you are going to help many women, just like you helped me," Amelia praised Melissa. Melissa responded with a little blush.

"I'm so glad I was able to help you, Amelia. I just wish it had been sooner," Melissa said seriously and compassionately.

"I wish it had been sooner too. But something good is going to come of this. I'm going to focus on helping women too. Crazy, isn't it? I never thought I would be doing this, but the heart wants, what the heart wants," Amelia said, pride visible on her face.

"That's wonderful! You are right, the heart wants what the heart wants," Melissa repeated with an incredible look on her face Amelia could not interpret.

"Well, I better get going. I've got to get back to the office before Sandra has a fit. Again, it's good to see you Melissa, take care." Amelia said, turning to walk away.

"Hey Amelia. Would you like to get coffee sometime? Can I give you a call?" Melissa asked, a tentative look on her face.

"I'd love that. Call me anytime, you have my number, I'll see you soon, Bye!" Amelia said and walked away. Heading to her car Amelia was giddy. Why was she giddy? Was it because she had just registered for her classes or because she had seen Melissa? She didn't think about it much, as she got in her car, and drove back to work.

Minutes before closing the office, Amelia reached into her jacket pocket for a tissue, when she found Melissa's new business card. She read it, and notice the bottom of her card, it read, **"Let us help you live again, love again, dream again."** Amelia's mind was a little confused. It was the same thing written on the stationery in the red envelope she had received.

Her mind was perplexed. She asked herself, 'Is Melissa the mystery writer of the letters?' She thought about it and starting putting clues together. The fountain pen, the statements during court that matched the letters, the way Melissa had looked at her on occasion. Could it be? The more Amelia thought about it, the more sense it made to Amelia. But Melissa knew that Amelia was straight, right?

Amelia shrugged it off, just thinking that Melissa just couldn't be the writer of the letters. She just couldn't believe it. She decided to just let it be and see if anything else gave her any clues.

CHAPTER 8

Four months had passed since the trial, and Amelia's life was her own. She was doing well in her classes. Her business was even more successful now that she could focus on it. The only thing, she could not force herself to date. She had tried. Three male agents from other agencies had asked her out, but something kept holding her back.

Amelia was busy at work when her cell phone rang. She looked at it and didn't recognize the number but decided to answer it anyway.

"Amelia Thomson at the Thomson Ackers Insurance Agency speaking," she answered thinking it was a work call.

"Hi Amelia, it's Melissa Garner. How are you?" Melissa said on the line. Amelia's heart jumped a little and she instantly smiled.

"Hi Melissa, I'm great. So good to hear from you. How is the law firm?" she asked, curious as to her success.

"Oh, it's going great. That's one of the reasons I called you. I was wondering if you could meet me for coffee, and so we can talk about an idea I have that I think would be right for you," Melissa said, without details.

"Sure Melissa, just tell me when and where. I'll be there," Amelia said, knowing she was looking forward to seeing Melissa and to hearing about her idea.

"Well, how about I text you the date/time, and place. It may be in a couple of days. Is that okay?" Melissa said with excitement in her voice.

"Absolutely. I don't have any appointments next week so far, and my classes are at night. My daily schedule is flexible. Just let me know. I'm looking forward to seeing you," Amelia said, with a sense of excitement and intrigue.

"Sounds great, see you soon, bye," Melissa said, and hung up. Amelia held the phone for another few seconds before hanging up. Thoughts of intrigue and excitement and something else she didn't quite recognize. She would have to wait and see.

CHAPTER 9

True to her word, Melissa texted Amelia three days later, and they decided to meet at 10am on Friday at Jimmy's Café and Eatery on the south end of Dorchester Road. It was about a 20-minute ride from Amelia's work, but Sandra didn't mind being the main agent now that they had hired a part-time receptionist.

Friday came quickly, and Amelia left work at 930am, knowing morning traffic in Charleston could be crazy. Luckily, she arrived at Jimmy's Café and Eatery with 10 minutes to spare. She parked and walked into the café, ordered coffee and pastry, and found a seat. A few minutes later, Melissa walked in and saw Amelia right away. She went ahead and ordered her coffee, grabbed a pastry, and walked to their table.

"Amelia, so good to see you," Melissa said, as she hugged Amelia when she stood up to greet her. Amelia hugged her back and felt a warmth she had not felt before.

Sitting down, Amelia could not wipe the smile off her face as she looked at Melissa's hazel eyes. She noticed how Melissa's blond hair framed her face, cascaded over her shoulders and down her back. Her lips full, with pink lipstick.

Melissa smiled and looked at Amelia, noticing her dark eyes. She noticed Amelia's deep brown hair up in a French braid that accented Amelia's strong chin, delicate ears, and sensuous neck. Melissa was having a challenging time not staring. Remembering why they were there brought Melissa back to Earth.

"Well, I'm glad you are here. I had hoped you wouldn't be too busy to meet me. I know your agency has grown like crazy. I saw the article the local Chamber did on your agency, and I was impressed." Melissa said, so proud of what Amelia had been able to do in such a short amount of time.

"Melissa, that is so sweet of you. The article came at the right time. I was so surprised when they asked us about doing the article on our agency. I had no idea if anyone really knew who we were. But I understand they got a couple of calls from customers, complimenting us on our involvement in our community with women in need, and in support of women and families. I count us blessed and lucky to have gotten that boost," Amelia said humbly.

"I think it's phenomenal. You so much deserve it. Your work in such a short amount of time has been incredible," Melissa said, having heard nothing but positive things from community leaders.

"The reason I wanted to talk to you, is that our firm has decided to do something different. We specialize in women and families, domestic partner violence, and women's advocacy. After talking with other agencies, social workers, and other specialists, we have decided to hire a Client Advocate. The Client Advocate will be helping our clients find the resources they need in the community, while our firm helps them legally. Right now, we are having to use our time doing the resource calling on top of the legal work, which limits us as to how many clients we can help. What do you think of the idea?" Melissa queried Amelia.

Amelia responded enthusiastically, "What a great idea. Having ready resource contacts available helps clients get help quicker and frees up their time to help others. A win/win for everyone." Amelia's smile widened.

"Well, after I thought of the idea, I thought of you. I know you volunteer at the help line, and you are working toward your social work degree. This would give you real life experience and prepare you for what you could do after graduating." Melissa explained, hoping Amelia would see the opportunity.

"Melissa, I love the idea, but I'm not sure I could fit it into my schedule at work. We are so busy right now, I'm not sure I could dump anymore of the work on Sandra," Amelia said with concern in her voice.

"I understand Amelia. I was hoping you could see that you could do this instead of being an insurance agent. I've already talked to other law firms that specialize like we do, and they have all agreed the idea is great. Your position would be split between all the firms, with each one paying you separately. The salary would be much more than what you are earning now. You could work out of any firm or office you wanted, and you would be supported with office staff as well to help you. We already have a list of clients for you, and the firms are really motivated to make this work, as it will free up resources at each firm." Melissa concluded, looking, and sounding positive, knowing this was perfect for Amelia.

Amelia couldn't believe she was being offered such an incredible opportunity. She was excited, but really felt like she needed to think on it to make sure it was what she wanted.

"Melissa, it all sounds so fantastic. I really need some time to think about it. It's such a huge step for me, and I need to make sure it's the right thing for me to do. How soon do you need an answer?" Amelia asked anxiously.

"As soon as you can get back to me. We have a list of twenty clients for you now. If you don't want this position, we will have to find someone else," Melissa said, concern in her voice and on her face.

"Let me think about it over the weekend. I can call you on Monday and let you know. I have a lot to think about," Amelia said tentatively. Her mind reeling at the opportunity.

"That's perfect Amelia. I hope you decide to do this. I think it's perfect for you." Melissa said, smiling encouragement at Amelia, hoping with all hope Amelia would say yes.

After finishing their coffee and conversation they said their goodbyes, and both left the café. Amelia was thinking about the opportunity, and Melissa was thinking about Amelia.

CHAPTER 10

Week after week, Amelia received a red envelope with a letter. Every day when Amelia got home, she would park her car, walk to the mailbox, and check to see if there was a red envelope for her. It had become intriguing; she could hardly hold her excitement.

The last two read,

"Open your heart, open your mind, your future is here. Opportunities knock but once. Whether love or work, neither will wait."

"Acquaintances to friends to lovers, open your heart, see more. Let your heart rule; as your mind may be confused, but your heart always knows the truth."

She thought about what they said. Why did they always know what she was thinking? It was almost scary. But deep down inside, she knew what they said was true.

The opportunity that Melissa and the other attorneys and firms had offered her was incredible. She would be working in her field of study, be able to help people from day one. She would have support staff to help her and could choose where she wanted her office to be. But she had to give up her insurance agency. She needed to talk to Sandra, to get her take on the opportunity.

Amelia called Sandra and asked if she had time to meet for dinner after work. Sandra said yes, and that her husband wouldn't be home tonight since he was on the road delivering equipment and wouldn't return for several days.

At 530pm Sandra and Amelia met at the Dorchester Diner. After ordering drinks and dinner, Amelia decided to tell Sandra about the opportunity.

"Sandra, I wanted to talk to you because I have been presented with an incredible opportunity, and I'm not sure I can turn it down. But I want to talk to you about it before I make up my mind," Amelia said tentatively looking at Sandra.

"Okay, what is it, you are making me nervous," Sandra said, sitting on the edge of her seat.

"Well, you know I'm in school at night for a social work degree. Melissa Garner, the former assistant district attorney started her own firm with a friend, and they specialize in women and family advocacy. She has talked to other firms that also use their resources to help these women and families. They have decided to hire a Client Advocate to help the women and families find the resources they need, while the attorneys work on the legal cases. That way the firms can help more people and use less resources. The thing is, Melissa offered me the job," Amelia said, watching Sandra close for her reaction.

"Amelia, that's wonderful. I think you would be perfect for it. You already volunteer at the phone bank on the weekends, and at the shelter, so you are familiar with the resources that are available. Why are you hesitating?" Sandra asked, putting a hand on Amelia's arm in concern.

"Sandra, it would mean I would have to give up the agency. This position would be a full-time position, with a huge salary and support staff. But my concern is you, and how my leaving would affect you," Amelia said with concern in her voice, and on her face.

"Well, you don't have to worry about that. My Henry is on

the road right now, but last month he took his insurance licensing exam. I could bring him into the office full time and get him off the road. He is exceptionally good at helping people and is computer literate. I don't think it will take long for him to get up to speed. I don't want you to worry about that. Why don't you let Henry, and I buy you out of the agency, that way you can have extra money put aside. Otherwise, we would have to give you a residual until we reached the agreed amount. What do you think of that?" Sandra said, all excited that she had a ready solution for Amelia and herself.

"Oh, Sandra, that is perfect. I just didn't want to leave you without knowing there was a plan in place. I just don't feel like I can turn this opportunity down. Are you sure you and Henry can buy me out?" Amelia asked, knowing they'd had money problems in the past.

"No problem. Henry can sell his truck, and we can pay you from that," Sandra said, knowing this was the right thing to do.

"Well, you talk to Henry and let me know by Sunday. I need to let Melissa know on Monday what my decision, hopefully that gives you enough time." Amelia said,

"That's plenty of time as a matter of fact. I'll call him as soon as I get home. I'm sure he'll agree since he's been wanting to get off the road for quite some time." Sandra said, pleased that she and Henry would be building something together.

"Sounds like we have agreed then. I'll wait for your call this weekend, and then I'll let Melissa know on Monday. Thank you, Sandra. You have made me feel so much better about this decision. Let's make sure we stay in contact. You have been such a good friend; I wouldn't want anything to come between us." Amelia said seriously.

"I would never let that happen; we will be good friends forever. I remember when we first met, and you hired me to help you. I remember when you made me a full partner. This opportunity is too good for you to turn down. I would be foolish to get in your way. Let's just make sure to communicate with each other as much as possible. You know you are still invited to our house for major holidays, just like we've done for years. Nothing will change," Sandra said sincerely, looking forward to seeing Amelia grow into her new job. She also hoped Amelia would find love too. But she knew that was not under anyone's control.

As they finished dinner, and left to go home, Amelia was excited to be able to tell Melissa yes, on Monday. She was also a little excited to be working close to Melissa. She guessed it was because they were familiar with each other, as she couldn't think of any other reason.

CHAPTER 11

Monday morning, after breakfast, Amelia called Melissa. Melissa answered on the second ring, as if anticipating Amelia's call.

"Melissa Garner speaking," Melissa said, in her professional tone.

"Hi Melissa, it's Amelia. How are you this morning?" Amelia asked, a little nervous and extremely excited.

"Amelia, I'm great. How are you?" Melissa asked, a little excitement notable in her voice.

"I'm great thanks. I have an answer for you, Melissa. The answer is yes. I'll take that position," Amelia said, excitement and pride in her voice and on her face.

"Oh Amelia, wonderful! I'm so proud of you for making such a major decision so quickly. How much time will you need to settle your affairs at the agency?" Melissa asked, knowing there was work Amelia would have to do before coming on full-time.

"Sandra and I worked it out. I can start next week. Her husband is going to be collaborating with her at the agency, and they are buying me out. I will be able to start bright and early next Monday," Amelia said, excited and motivated.

"That's great Amelia. If you can come here on Wednesday, I can show you your office and introduce you to the support staff. We can have lunch if you can come at 1pm. I've got to be in court at 230, so I won't have a lot of time," Melissa said, hoping Amelia would say yes to the time and lunch.

"That's perfect Melissa. I'm so excited. I look forward to

seeing you on Wednesday at 1pm. See you then," Amelia finished.

"See you then," Melissa said, with an odd tone to her voice. Amelia couldn't decide if Melissa was excited, or what; she just couldn't place the tone in her voice.

Wednesday came quickly, and Amelia was extremely excited to take the first step to her new future. She turned out of her office and headed towards Melissa's firm. Her heart jumped a little every time she thought about Melissa. She just couldn't understand why.

20 minutes later she was pulling into the parking lot of Garner and Brooks, Attorneys at Law. She stepped out of the car and walked towards the door of a stylish building with big Palladian windows that most certainly enhanced the lighting inside.

As she opened the door to go into the firm, a woman, and her son, walked out and bumped into Amelia. Amelia could see the woman had been crying.

"Ma'am, are you okay? Is there anything I can help you with?" Amelia instinctively said, suspecting this might be someone she might could help.

"I'm okay, I guess. I just met with my lawyer. Ms. Brooks is helping me get a divorce, but I'm upset because we don't have a place to stay tonight." The lady was visibly upset, and the little boy seemed tired and upset too.

"Did you let your lawyer know your circumstance?" Amelia asked, hoping they had tried to help her.

"Well, no. I didn't think they could help me with that," the distraught woman said. It was obvious she had said nothing to her attorney.

Amelia reached into her purse and withdrew a business

card. "Here, let me give you this business card, it's to the Women's and Family Shelter. They can help you. Just call them, tell them your situation. They will give you a reference number, and an address to report to. When you get to that address, enter the reference number into the security gate, and it will let you in. Then someone will meet you in the office to take you where you need to be. It's very secure, and they have resources to help you there," Amelia said, familiar with the agency she was talking about, as she had referred women there already.

"Oh my gosh, thank you so much. I never thought we would need help, but I'm so glad I met you today. What is your name please?" The lady asked, the distraught look slowly easing from her face.

"My name is Amelia Thomson. I'm the new Client Advocate here, and I'll be helping women and families with resources they may need. If you need anything at all, just call the main number here, and they will transfer you to me," Amelia said confidently, knowing she was ready for this.

"I will Amelia. It's such a pleasure to meet you. Thank you for your help. I feel better already," the lady said, a big smile on her face.

"Well, you be safe on the road. I'm sure I'll be talking to you soon," Amelia said, as they parted, and she entered the law firm.

Amelia's heart felt good, she had been able to help someone, and she hadn't even started her first day. It put a big smile on her face and gave her heart a lift.

As she entered the firm, she noticed the décor and colors, they seemed soothing. The large windows lighting up each room. The receptionist was an older woman, and she noticed Amelia as soon as she walked in.

"Hello, welcome to Garner and Brooks. How may I assist you today?" the receptionist said, genuinely smiling at Amelia.

"Hi, I'm Amelia Thomson, Melissa Garner is expecting me," Amelia said, returning the smile.

"Oh yes, welcome Amelia. Melissa has told us so much about you. She is so impressed by you. We feel like we know you by now," the receptionist said, taking Amelia by surprise.

What exactly had Melissa said? This was an intriguing situation.

"Melissa is on a call right now, but she should be finished shortly. Let me take you into her sitting area, and you can wait there," the receptionist rose from her desk and motioned for Amelia to follow her.

Down the hallway, the receptionist ushered her into a sitting room that looked more like a living room. She told her Melissa's office was thru the door on the left, and the private bathroom was to the right. Then before she left, she offered her something to drink, but Amelia refused and thanked her.

After the receptionist left, Amelia walked around the sitting room and noticed the pictures on the wall. She saw Melissa standing with clients, and some families. She also saw pictures of Melissa getting awards. Then further down the other wall, the awards Melissa had received were displayed; plaques and certificates covered the wall. It was obvious that Melissa cared deeply about people.

Amelia had her own personal proof of that. Every time she had met or spoken with Melissa; Amelia had felt the genuine warmth that came from her...it gave her a sense of comfort.

Still looking at the awards, she was unaware of the office door opening.

"I see you have found my wall of fame," Melissa said, a smile on her face, and joking tone in her voice.

A little surprised by Melissa's silent approach, Amelia quickly turned and smile at Melissa, when she heard her voice.

Chuckling, Amelia replied, "it's obviously a ploy to enchant possible clients into thinking you're a hot shot attorney." Amelia and Melissa laughed lightly.

"Really, so that's what you think of me," Melissa replied, still joking with Amelia.

"Of course, I know first-hand what you can do," Amelia said, remembering how Melissa had rescued her, and helped turn her life around.

"Well, I think you are worth it, don't you?" Melissa asked, an unusual look on her face, and a glint in her eyes.

"I hope so. We'll find out over the next few months," Amelia said, her heart fluttering at the thought of spending time with Melissa.

"Yes, we will, Let's go into my office and talk more about the position, and then I'll walk you to your office, and introduce you to everyone. Though, I must tell you, I've been talking you up to everyone. So don't be surprised, okay?" Melissa said, sounding proud of herself.

"So, I've found out already, as soon as I came in," Amelia smiled as they walked into Melissa's office.

"Rachel talked to you already, didn't she?" Melissa asked, as she rounded her desk to sit down.

"Yes, Rachel told me you had already told her about me. I found it odd, but comforting all at the same time," Amelia said with a small chuckle, and a smile on her face, as she looked into Melissa's hazel eyes.

Melissa's cheeks warmed with a little embarrassment, knowing she should have waited until Amelia started. But she had been so ecstatic to find out Amelia would be working with them in the office, that she had not been able to hold it back from her co-workers.

Over the next hour, Melissa explained exactly what Amelia would be doing, and gave her information on the other firms involved. The information had phone numbers, email addresses, and contacts for information that Amelia did not have already. She also handed Amelia a folder that listed the names of twenty clients the firms needed help with right away.

On Monday, Amelia would hit the ground running, trying to help twenty clients find their way in their new world. Then the real work would begin.

Melissa then took Amelia to meet everyone in the firm. First of course, she officially introduced Amelia to Rachel, the receptionist. They discussed schedules and resources Rachel could help Amelia with.

Then, Melissa introduced Amelia to Melissa's law partner, Kim Brooks, a tall brunette of Middle Eastern dissent. The plaques on the wall showed her name as Makhim Patel-Brooks, so she understood why everyone called her Kim Brooks.

"We are so glad to have you on board. Melissa has been talking about you all week."

Amelia responded, "Oh, thank you for having me. I'm looking forward to getting started Monday." While they were talking, Amelia noticed the wedding picture which had two brides. One was Kim in a flowing white dress, and there was a tall blond that only had eyes for Kim, wearing another flowing white dress.

"I see you noticed my wedding day picture. That's my wife Robin. We've been married five years. She is a doctor at the local hospital. You'll meet her soon as she comes by the office from time to time." Kim said without any thought as to how Amelia would react.

Amelia knew that Melissa was gay, but she had not thought anything when Melissa had said she had a law partner. The thought that she would be working with two lesbians did not affect Amelia, but it did make her think back to her college days.

"It's a lovely picture. You look so happy and in love. Congratulations," Amelia said sincerely, noticing the smile on Kim's face.

"Thank you, Amelia. I appreciate that." Kim said sincerely.

"Okay, Amelia, let's go meet the support staff," Melissa interrupted, standing up and beginning to leave the office.

"Kim, I'm so looking forward to working with you. See you soon," Amelia said, smiling at Kim, as she left the office following Melissa.

Walking down another hall into a huge room, Melissa said, "this will be your office, and reception area. We have the carpenters coming this weekend to put up a divider wall and add an outside entrance. We want to make sure you have a private office for yourself. And, that reception will have enough room. Your receptionist will be here as well, so when people come in from the outside, she will be able to see them right away. Also, there are two side offices for your two assistants that will be helping you once you come on board. We have not hired them because we want you to hire your own people." Melissa finished talking, turned, and looked at Amelia. Melissa stared at Amelia's dark eyes, holding her look longer than usual before she looked away.

Amelia did not know what to make of Melissa's stare, but it gave her goose bumps. Amelia looked away and turned to walk through the expansive room as a distraction.

"Wow, this is a vast area. Are you sure we are going to need all this room?" Amelia asked, trying to stay away from Melissa while she talked.

"Not in the beginning, but after talking to all the firms, we think you will be managing about one hundred women and families a month. So, you may have multiple people waiting for appointments for you. We wanted to make sure everyone would be comfortable." Mellisa said, noting how Amelia stayed away from her, not wanting to look at her face. Melisssa realized that she had stared too long at Amelia and felt embarrassed. She turned around in the opposite direction to clear the blush on her face. But she continued talking so as not to break the rhythm of conversation.

"Now I'll introduce you to the support staff. They are mostly administrative but can run errands if needed. They will be helping you until you get your assistants hired and trained. Anything you need done, just let them know, they've already been briefed," Melissa said, beginning to walk towards the door.

Amelia followed her but did not look at her face. It was like Amelia was afraid, Melissa thought. Melissa was a little afraid too.

Walking down the hall, past a nice kitchen, they entered a large office that contained two desks, which were currently occupied.

"Ladies, this is Amelia Thomson, the new client advocate I've been telling you about. Amelia this is Liz, she manages legal paperwork and court filings," Melissa said, as she walked toward

Liz. Amelia stepped forward and shook Liz's hand. She found her grip firm, but friendly. Liz's face smiled a friendly smile too. Her eyes showing genuine interest.

"Hi Amelia. We've heard so much about you. We are all looking forward to working with you," Liz said, smiling brightly at Amelia as if she were smiling at a friend. It made Amelia feel like she was among family.

"And this is Becca, she helps manage phones, non-legal paperwork, and is great at running errands, and keeping us on schedule to court," Melissa said with great admiration.

"Welcome Amelia," Becca said, as she came around from her desk and offered her hand. Amelia shook Becca's hand and knew she would get along with Becca just fine.

"Anything you need, just let me know. I'm the general do-everything around here. I try to keep everyone straight, which is an impossible task, believe me," Becca said, laughing and joking.

"That will never happen," Melissa said, joking back. The joke was going right over Amelia. It wasn't until later that Amelia would find out what that meant.

Melissa led Amelia back to her office, and she said, "Looks like we won't be able to make lunch today, as it's taken us too long. But if you have time, would you like to meet for dinner after work?" Melissa asked, hoping Amelia would say yes.

Overwhelmed with all the new people and information, Amelia was hesitant to say yes. She also had to get back to the agency and didn't know whether she had to work late.

"Would you mind if we have dinner another day. I don't know if I'm going to have to work late at the agency, since I've been gone so long?" Amelia said innocently and honestly, knowing how she felt right now.

Disappointed by Amelia's response, but understanding today had covered a lot, Melissa responded, "that sounds like a good idea. Why don't we wait until you get settled in, and get things running first," Melissa said.

Then she added, "I know you must get back to the agency, and I must be in court in 20 minutes. So, I'm going to walk out with you," Melissa said, picking up her briefcase, purse, and keys off her credenza. She then began to walk out with Amelia towards the door, passing Rachel's desk.

"Rachel, I'm headed to court. I'll call you if I'm going to be running late," Melissa said as she passed Rachel at her desk.

"Okay boss. Pleasure to meet you, Amelia. We'll see you on Monday" Rachel said in a friendly tone, as both Amelia and Melissa walked out of the office and into the parking lot.

"Hope the rest of your day goes great," Melissa said, as Amelia reached her car.

"You too, Melissa. Thanks for everything today. See you Monday, bright and early," Amelia responded, opening her car door, and sitting down. As she started her car, she saw Melissa drive off.

Amelia thought, I know I did not imagine that look that Melissa gave me. What was that about? Amelia could still not fathom what she was feeling, or how Melissa made her feel.

As she drove back to the agency, her mind churned the emotions running through it, as did her heart.

It took Amelia 30 minutes to reach her agency parking lot, as traffic had started to pick up. She left her car and entered the office. Sandra was on the phone as Amelia approached her desk. As soon as she hung up, Sandra went into questions mode.

"How did it go Amelia?" "Was everyone nice?" "What

did y'all talk about?," Sandra said, before Amelia could even answer the first question. Amelia laughed lightly, turned on her computer, and waited to see if Sandra was going to ask for anything else.

Seconds later, Amelia answered, "it went great. Everyone was genuinely nice. The offices are beautiful. And I helped a client out even before I got there," Amelia said, then went on to explain to Sandra what had happened.

As she finished explaining, Amelia remembered the conversations with each person she had met at the firm. She also remembered the way Melissa had looked at her, and how it had made her feel...excited!

Not hearing Sandra talk, Amelia tried to resolve the conflict between Melissa's stare and her feelings.

"Amelia? Amelia? Are you listening to me?" Amelia finally heard Sandra asking loudly.

"I'm sorry Sandra. It's been a long day, and I'm tired," Amelia said, trying to persuade herself and Sandra everything was okay. But her mind kept thinking of that stare, and her body was warming to the memory.

"Well, why don't you go ahead and head home. You got here early, and there is nothing important you need to finish. Henry is coming tomorrow to start learning the paperwork, so he can help while you finish anything tomorrow. Friday, we can train him on the computer. He is such a whiz; he'll catch on quick." Sandra said, concerned about Amelia and the look on her face.

"I think I'll take you up on that if you are sure, you don't need me," she said to Sandra.

"No, I can manage anything in the next two hours before we close. Go and relax, I've got this," Sandra assured Amelia. She smiled as she saw Amelia turn her computer off, grab her purse, and head for the door with keys in hand.

"All right, I'll see you tomorrow. Call me if anything comes up. And thanks Sandra. I appreciate you looking out for me." Amelia said in a sincere tone.

"After everything you've done for me and Henry, I owe you big time," Sandra said, knowing she owed everything to Amelia.

"You don't owe me anything Sandra. You've worked hard to become certified, helped me increase business, and the clients love you. If anything, I owe you for making me look so good," Amelia said smiling at Sandra. Her heart held Sandra in great esteem.

"Get out of here, before you embarrass me," Sandra jokingly said, watching Amelia exit.

Getting in her car, Amelia was looking forward to getting home early. Driving home, Amelia thought about her day, and how starting Monday her life would be changed forever. It made her happy, and she hoped that the change would be good for her mind, body, and soul. She hoped the change would help her truly heal from everything she had gone through and be a new and happy chapter in her life.

Arriving home, Amelia pulled into her driveway, turned off her car and exited. She walked to her mailbox and retrieved its contents. More junk as usual, but she noticed another red envelope sticking out from behind the junk. She grabbed the red envelope separating it from the other mail and held onto it as she entered her house. After entering, setting her keys and purse down, Amelia's excitement at receiving another red envelope could not be contained. She sat down on the couch and opened the envelope. Another red rose stationery unfolded, and she read its content,

"Soon, a new opportunity will lead you to eventual happiness and love. Your mind may not recognize it, but your heart will. Accept it!"

Strange, Amelia thought to herself. She read the writing again, and her mind went to Melissa. Why? She asked herself. She just could not understand, yet.

CHAPTER 12

It was Amelia's first full day as a Client Advocate. She had arrived 15 minutes early and found everyone was already at work. She spotted Rachel coming out of Melissa's office.

"Hi Rachel, does everyone automatically come in early, or did I miss something?" she asked Rachel, hoping she had not missed anything.

"Your good Amelia, we had a staff meeting this morning, preparing for a major case coming up. Melissa wanted us all early so she could go over information with all of us at the same time. It makes it easier for us to help her, and to keep up with changes when they happens." Rachel said, chuckling as she saw Amelia's distress at thinking she had missed something.

"Well, I'm glad I didn't miss anything, it would be a bad start to my first day," Amelia said, chuckling back at Rachel.

"I promise, if we needed you in on the meeting, I would have called you yesterday to let you know," Melissa spoke from behind Amelia, scaring her so much she jumped.

"Jeez, where did you come from? You sure can sneak up on someone. That's the second time you've done that to me," Amelia said joking, as she smiled at Melissa.

"Yeah, everyone around here says I move like a ghost, must be my childhood ballerina training," Melissa said, chuckling back at Amelia.

"Yep, that would do it I guess, I had better get to work ladies, I'll see you later," Amelia said as she started to walk toward her new office.

Melissa followed her down the hallway.

"Stalking me already, huh?" Amelia said, as she realized Melissa was behind her.

"I don't resort to stalking until we've been in a relationship at least a year," Melissa laughed.

Amelia knew it was a joke, but her heart and body responded to the word relationship. She had no idea why, but she was getting that warming sensation in her body again.

"Just wanted to let you know that if you need anything, don't be afraid to ask Rachel or me, or anyone for that matter. We all want you to succeed," Melissa said, looking intently at Amelia, that glint in her eyes.

"I won't be afraid to ask for anything. I just hope I can perform to everyone's standards," Amelia said, feeling a little subconscious.

"The only standard you must perform to is your own. Remember, I believe in you, and I know you can do this. Just take your time getting to know the system, ask questions, and always remember we care," Melissa said, a caring look on her face as she looked with intent at Amelia.

Amelia's heart jumped a little at Melissa's look. She saw Melissa's lips, and her eyes, and the way Melissa looked at her, and her heart yelled at her, "desire." What? Amelia shook her head slightly and thought, 'No way!'

"Are you okay Amelia?" Melissa asked, a concerned look on her face as she watched Amelia.

"I'm good Melissa, just anxious to get started. I have a lot to learn," Amelia said, trying to avert her gaze, as she set her purse and keys down on her desk, and looked around.

"Okay, I'll leave you to it. Just remember to take breaks and eat lunch. We don't want you passing out on your first day. I'll talk to you later," Melissa said as she turned around and walked back to her own office.

Amelia sat in her chair, turned it around toward the wall. Her mind was churning everything. Amelia could not get the picture of Melissa's lips, eyes, and facial expression out of her mind. Her heart yelled at her again, "desire."

Oh god, I'm hallucinating, Amelia thought. "Enough" she muttered to herself, turned her chair back around and turned on her computer. She had to get to work, or her mind would keep churning all day.

CHAPTER 13

The weeks seemed to fly by. In the office by 830am, Monday through Friday; classes at night, 2 days a week- Tuesday and Thursday. Every day something new, never dull. Amelia was loving it.

Her days were full and happy, her nights filled with dreams. Several times a week, Amelia would dream of the faceless woman making love to her. She would wake near orgasm often, and just couldn't get the image, feelings, or thoughts out of her mind. It was slowly driving her crazy.

On top of everything, she had received four letters in these weeks since she had started her new job. They intrigued her more and more. She remembered what they said,

"Do you see what I see when you look in the mirror...a pure heart ready to share its love. Open your heart to all the possibilities; love is there, prepare your heart."

"Passion, love, longing...all related to that feeling in your heart. Open your heart, open your mind, feel it!"

"Every heart knows when it is in love; the difference is quieting the doubts in our minds."

With only two appointments in the morning, and two after lunch, she decided to check in with Melissa to see if they could finally have that dinner. It would be nice to catch up, as they had both been so busy, they often just passed each other in the hallway.

Amelia got up the nerve, called Rachel to see if Melissa was free. Rachel said yes, so Amelia walked into the other part of the building and headed to Melissa's office.

After knocking, and hearing Melissa say, "come in," Amelia opened the door a fraction, stuck her head in, and asked, "hi Melissa, you got a minute?"

"Of course I do. Come in, I feel like we are like ships passing in the night," Melissa joked with Amelia and pointed at the chair so she could sit down.

"How is it going? I hear from the other firms you are doing outstanding work. They are incredibly happy." Melissa said, proud of Amelia.

"That's great to hear Melissa. It's been a whirlwind I can tell you that. But now that I have help, things are getting into a routine, so I can begin to relax a little," Amelia said. She had hired two assistants this last week, and they had been able to pick up speed very quickly.

"Yes, your new assistants, Darlene and Carla are impressive! I'm so glad you had the forethought to hire from your group of classmates and volunteers. What a great idea!" Melissa said, getting out of her chair, walking to her credenza, and pouring herself some water.

"Would you like some water," Melissa asked Amelia, without turning around to look at her. What she didn't see is Amelia studying the curve of her body, the length of her legs, and the style of her hair.

Amelia answered Melissa, "Yes, please," after she realized she had not answered her right away. She had been looking at Melissa's back, her eyes roving of their own volition. That warm feeling returning and seemed to be magnified. As Melissa turned around, Amelia looking away. Then she saw Melissa passing the glass to Amelia.

Amelia's fingers touched Melissa's. You would have thought they were both struck by lightning, as a bolt of energy ran through Amelia's fingers. She was sure Melissa had felt it too. She quickly pulled the glass from Melissa's hands, keeping her eyes down at the glass.

As Amelia drank her water, her eyes closed, Melissa's image in her mind. When she opened her eyes, Melissa was giving her that look. "That look" had become Melissa's calling card to Amelia: when they talked, when they met, when they passed in the hallway. Amelia had no idea what that look meant, but she knew how it made her feel. And she liked it!

"I came by to see if you wanted to meet for lunch or dinner. I seem to remember that you owe me one," Amelia said, a joking smirk on her face.

"Oh, that's right. We said we would put it off until you were settled. To be honest, I had forgotten all about it. I think that would be great. When would you like to go?" Melissa asked, looking down at her calendar, waiting for Amelia response. She saw how nervous Amelia was, so she wanted to give her a minute to get herself together.

Amelia's heart skipped a beat, when she saw Melissa look down, so she couldn't see the look on Amelia's face when she noticed Melissa's cleavage. *'Holy Mother of God!'* Amelia thought to herself. *'What is wrong with me?'* Amelia could see the curve of Melissa's breasts peep from the lacy bra and out through the slightly unbuttoned blouse. She asked herself, 'Why did I look?' She had no answer, but she knew her body was reacting positively, and she had no idea how to get it under control.

Amelia answered Melissa's question, finally looking up, "at

your convenience. I have time over the weekend if you do." Her heart hoping Melissa said yes, her body not knowing what she was doing.

"Yeah, that sounds great. I'm free this weekend. How about dinner on Saturday? Are you into seafood," Melissa asked, hoping that Amelia said yes. Her mind was hoping, and her body feeling the need to be near Amelia.

"That sounds good. I love seafood," Amelia responded, her mind already looking forward to Saturday.

"Let's meet about 3pm, an early dinner, then if you want to, we can go to the river and walk the trail before sunset. It's so beautiful this time of year," Melissa said, her eyes lighting up with anticipation.

"That sounds great Melissa. Hey, have you ever been to Ronnie's at Folly Beach, it is so good, and their variety is wonderful," Amelia suggested, knowing it was not an intimate setting, which would make her feel better.

"Oooh! Ronnie's! I love their fried oysters and shrimp. Sounds great. How about I come by and pick you up, so we only take one car, I'll drive the convertible, and we can take advantage of the great weather," Melissa said, hoping Amelia would say yes.

"That's sounds fun," Amelia said, trying to convince herself that this was a work dinner, but her heart kept thinking this was turning into a date. Her mind decided to shelve the thoughts for now. Her excitement now visible on her face, lighting up like a spotlight had landed on her.

Melissa noticed Amelia's excitement and mirrored it. Melissa had been thinking a great deal about Amelia lately, and knew she wanted to get to know her better.

"Well, I had better get back to work, I have an appointment

in ten minutes. So, I'll see you later. Looking forward to Saturday," Amelia said, standing up and turning for the door.

"Me too," Melissa said, Amelia noticing the soft tone in her voice. It made Amelia's heart skip a beat and returned that warm feeling to her body. What Amelia didn't see was Melissa studying her body, back, and legs as she walked out. She highly approved.

Returning to her office, Amelia smiled to herself, but on the inside, she was a nervous wreck. The more Amelia thought about it, the more it affected her. Did she have feelings for Melissa? Where did this come from? Why was she thinking like this? She had no answers.

Luckily, a flurry of phone calls, and two appointments before lunch kept her mind busy. She had brought her lunch, so she went out to her car, put on the radio, and ate her lunch listening to her favorite music. Music always calmed her down.

Amelia loved listening to songs filled with love, laughter, and living. She had come to enjoy this so much, since she had never had the opportunity to listen much when she was married to Mark. Mark had always hated music. She remembered him saying that music was "too sappy," and "a waste of time."

Having eaten leftovers from last night, she nestled into her car seat. The sun warmed the inside of the car, and it was minutes before Amelia nodded off.

She was awakened by a tap on her car window. It was Melissa. Amelia was embarrassed, thinking she had gone over her hour lunch, but looking at the clock, she saw that she had 30 minutes left of her lunch hour.

She rolled down the window, and Melissa asked, "Are you okay Amelia?" Concern on Melissa's face was visible.

"I'm fine. I ate lunch, and the car got warm, I just nodded

off," Amelia said, as the blush on her cheeks began to calm down. She couldn't believe Melissa had caught her sleeping.

"Okay, just wanted to make sure you were okay. You looked so peaceful," Melissa said, seeing Amelia blush lightly. She smiled at Amelia and the blush deepened.

"Well with all the work, classes, and volunteering, I think I'm not getting enough sleep. But a little power nap is not a bad thing. Besides, I have my cell phone alarm set." Amelia tried to explain, feeling guilty for an unknown reason. After all, it was her lunch time.

"Now I know not to interrupt when you are at lunch in your car. Sorry. I wish I could sleep that soundly. I knocked on your window three times. I was afraid you were dead," Melissa said, a chuckle in her voice, and a light in her eye.

"Well, I'm glad I'm not!" Amelia laughed back, seeing the light in Melissa's eyes. It made her want to stare into those beautiful eyes. But she changed her visual direction and went to get out of the car.

"Oh gosh, I'm sorry Amelia. Please don't leave it on my account. I'll leave you alone so you can finish," Melissa said, feeling guilty for having interrupted Amelia's lunch nap.

"Oh, that's okay. I'm almost finished. I am going to wash my sleep out of my eyes before my next appointment. I'll see you later," Amelia said, as she locked up her car, and started walking to her office's entrance. She just could not keep staring at Melissa's eyes, her body was reacting strangely, and she didn't know how to control it.

CHAPTER 14

Promptly at 3pm on Saturday, Melissa pulled into Amelia's driveway, honked the horn, and watched as Amelia exited her home and walked to the car.

"Hi Melissa, how are you?" Amelia asked, as she got into the car. She had not even looked at Melissa yet, not wanting to show just how excited she was.

"Looking forward to some good food, good company, and a good time," Melissa said, as she pulled the BMW convertible into traffic, headed for Ronnie's Seafood near Folly Beach, about a 30-minute ride from Amelia's house.

With the top down, the radio up, and the warm air, Amelia and Melissa smiled. They quickly passed historic Charleston mansions and plantations, numerous shopping areas, and green forests on the way to Folly Beach.

Melissa drove confidently over the bridge at Wappoo Creek which allowed them to cross from Charleston to James Island. Here and there, they spotted salt marshes, white egrets, grey herons, and other birds feasting off the fish and crabs in the marshes. There were people crabbing too.

Minutes later they crossed over the bridge that separated James Island from Oak Island. The smell of the ocean was becoming more intense as they got closer. The proliferation of birds now included white herons, pelicans, and swallows that played in groups in the sky.

Then came the bridge that crossed over Oak Island Creek, and into the outskirts of Folly Beach. Another 10 minutes and they were parking at Ronnie's on Folly. The ocean on one side, and the estuary visible on the other side. What a sight!

As Melissa pulled into the parking lot at Ronnie's she hit the button for the convertible top to close. Then she opened her purse, took out a brush, and brushed her blonde hair while looking in the rear-view mirror. She noticed Amelia pull out a brush and brush her flowing brown hair.

She had a challenging time keeping her eyes averted from what she could see in the mirror. Amelia's eyes pulling her into their magnetic pool, her lips slightly parted wanting to be kissed, her jawline needing to be explored.

Pulling her gaze away from the mirror, Melissa got her purse and exited the car. At the same time, Amelia exited as well. Over the top of the car their gazes met. Looking away at the same time, they walked slowly to the entrance at Ronnie's. The restaurant was busy, and the music was loud on the inside. Melissa asked to be led to the upper deck, so they could have a chance at having a conversation.

Melissa followed Amelia up the three flights of stairs as the server led them to a table on the corner of the upper deck. Melissa noticed Amelia's back side, the curves and angles that made Melissa's heart skip a beat, and warmth to start rising. The server took them to visually the best seats in the house, as you could see the ocean on one side, the estuary on another side, and downtown Folly Beach too.

After ordering drinks, they talked about Charleston and their favorite places. Melissa enjoyed going to the winery and distillery, art galleries, and outdoor concerts. Amelia enjoyed touring the old mansions, the Battery, and the Market Square.

"I have to say, my favorite place in Charleston is Sullivan's

Island. I love walking on the beach, as you already know. It doesn't matter how cold or hot, that beach is perfect. Light waves to play in, enough wind to keep cool, and views of Charleston at night are incredible." Amelia said, smiling at Melissa then looking away, afraid of getting caught staring at those incredible hazel eyes. Amelia felt a warmth beginning to rise in her body but tried to ignore it.

Melissa looked at Amelia when she looked away. Amelia's jawline was incredible, those lips looked ready to be kissed, and her body was like a violin…ready to be played. But Melissa knew that may never happen. She decided to settle for friendship, great conversations, and the occasional meal and drinks. That would be enough for now.

"I enjoy Sullivan's Island, but there is something about Folly Beach that I really enjoy. When my mind isn't settled, I come out here and walk until I'm too tired to think anymore. The sea waves crashing playing their hypnotic song. The birds flying overhead communicating their urgency. The dolphins playing in the afternoons like a movie you want to watch repeatedly." Melissa said, pulling her gaze away from Amelia, as Amelia turned her head towards Melissa. Melissa was afraid to look Amelia in the eyes, thinking she might scare her off, which was the last thing she wanted to do.

Amelia had felt Melissa's gaze on her when she had looked away. Amelia was afraid of what she was feeling, so unsure of herself, her heart, her body, and her mind.

"Here is our dinner," Melissa said, as the server brought and served them dinner, and refilled their wine glasses. When she walked away, Melissa said with a smile on her face, "this is the best you can get on the island."

"I agree," Amelia said, smiling back at Melissa then sipping her wine, before eating a fried oyster. It was crisp on the outside, and so flavor filled on the inside. She devoured them, like she was ravenous.

"I see you like the oysters, you just ate them like they are going out of style," Melissa laughed, as she commented on Amelia's hunger.

"I love them so much, I can't ever seem to get enough of them," Amelia said, then continued, "every time I come here, I devour the oysters…it must be the sea air." Amelia gave Melissa a look that gave her pause.

Melissa's body reacted to the look Amelia gave her. Warmth started between her legs and enveloped the rest of her body quickly. She had never felt like this before. She was falling in love with Amelia so fast, but she knew Amelia was straight. She began to prepare her heart for pain.

Amelia's body was feeling the effects of being around Melissa. She felt a magnetic and hypnotic pull that she was fighting to control. The warmth in her body was quickly becoming unbearable heat and was enveloping her from head to toe. She decided to change the subject.

"I see you enjoy the food here too, you finished before me," Amelia chuckled, as she sipped the last of her wine.

"You about ready for that walk. We can walk off the calories we just consumed," Melissa said, laughing, knowing she didn't care about the calories. She cared about spending time with Amelia. But she also knew she needed to take it easy.

"Well, I'm ready. Let's pay and start that walk," Amelia said, as she handed the server her credit card.

"Amelia, I'm supposed to be paying. I had originally invited you, remember?" Melissa said, as the server quickly walked away.

"Melissa, I owe you. Since the first day I met you, you have done nothing but protect me, take care of me, and look out for me. And you didn't forget about me when the case was over. You got me my incredible job that I absolutely love. You have changed my life more than anyone ever. Taking care of this check is the least I can do to start repaying you for all you have done for me," Amelia said with great sincerity in her voice.

"You don't owe me a thing. I'm glad I was able to help you get your life back. Now you are flourishing and looking so happy. That is payment enough!" Melissa said with great emotion in her voice, as she looked at Amelia. Amelia felt the caring and sincerity from Melissa.

"Well, we had better get this walk started if we plan to get back to Charleston before it gets too late," Amelia said after signing the restaurant receipt, and standing up from the table.

"Yeah, I guess you are right," Melissa agreed and followed Amelia out of the restaurant.

They waited at the corner for the light to change, then they trekked to the beach across the street. Taking off their shoes, they started walking through the sand, then to the wave line of the ocean. The waves were light, so walking was easy, but the water was cold. Every time a wave crashed, they both tried to avoid getting their legs wet, so they wouldn't shiver. Sometimes they made it, but most of the time they didn't. By the time they got back, the sun was starting to set, and Melissa knew she would be driving them back in the dark. But she had a surprise for Amelia.

"Come on Amelia. It looks like we are going to be driving back in the dark," Melissa encouraged Amelia to pick up her pace as they starting walking back to the car.

"We are going to make one stop on the way back, it won't take but a few minutes," Melissa said, as she unlocked the car, and opened the door.

"Okay, sounds good," Amelia said, her smile conveying happiness. Amelia had not been this happy since…she was a little girl. So many wasted years. She didn't want to waste another moment thinking about the past.

Melissa waited for Amelia to settle back into her seat, put her seat belt on before she pulled the powerful car out of the parking lot.

The afternoon had cooled off as the sun started setting, so Melissa didn't lower the top. Instead, she kept stealing glances at Amelia, feeling happy.

Heading back to Charleston, Melissa veered off Folly Road at the junction and took Hwy 30 towards Albemarle Point. Amelia didn't know it, but she was going to be able to see the sunset from the lighthouse on Albemarle Point at the Ashley River just north of the McLeod Plantation.

The gentleman that tended the lighthouse was a family friend of Melissa's and she had already called and arranged for them to have free reign of the lighthouse until after the sun went down. The lighthouse had been updated, and now automatically came on when the sun set, the time pre-programmed into the computer that controlled the light.

Melissa pulled into the parking lot, and said, "come on Amelia, let's go watch the sunset from the lighthouse." The surprised look from Amelia was more than worth all the effort Melissa had gone through.

"This is wonderful. I love lighthouses," Amelia exclaimed, following Melissa towards the door.

As they climbed the staircase headed up to the light and outside deck and railing, Amelia was excited and intrigued. Why had Melissa gone through so much trouble for her? Her heart skipped a beat as she thought about it. Nearing the top, she noticed it was a giant glass dome. The lens of the light was not on, as it was still light outside. So, they stepped out onto the observation deck, and the ocean breeze caught them. Tossing their hair and beginning to chill them, though neither cared.

Amelia was elated as she looked up to the sky, watching it turn pink, peach, orange, and shades of deep red, right before her eyes, as the sun reached the horizon on the Earth and reflected its light off the clouds. She gasped at the sheer beauty.

Melissa idled up to Amelia's side on the rail. Their arms barely touched as they both looked up into the sky in wonderment. Immediately, Amelia felt Melissa's warmth next to her body. She could feel the powerful magnetic force.

Melissa felt it too, but she knew she was powerless to do anything, otherwise she knew she would scare Amelia away…the one thing she did not want to do.

"When I was a little girl, my dad brought me here every time we went to the beach. I purposely delayed us leaving the beach, just so I could see the sunset from here. I can't get enough of it," Melissa said, looking at the setting sun, then stealing a sideways glance at Amelia.

"I can see why, this is the best view of the sunset I've ever seen," Amelia said, noticing the quick glance from Melissa.

She put her hand on Melissa's arm and said, "thank you for sharing this with me. It's wonderful," Amelia looked at Melissa's eyes, seeing the emotion that they contained. Amelia's heart was pounding in her chest as they looked at each other.

"I'm glad we had the time to do this. I'm glad you enjoyed it today," Melissa said, knowing by the look on Amelia's face that she had enjoyed today.

"We better start down the stairs before it gets too dark, and the light comes on. It will blind us…believe me I know." Melissa chuckled as she turned away from Amelia and started toward the stairs inside. Amelia followed. Their footsteps could be heard on the stairs inside of the lighthouse. Before they reached the bottom, the big light came on, and the brightness of it intimidated and intrigued Amelia.

Stepping outside and locking the door, Amelia and Melissa stopped for a moment and looked up at the giant light as it pierced the darkness over the ocean like a laser. It was as if God himself had opened the heavens and cast a light onto the ocean. It made them both gasp at the magnificent sight.

Simultaneously, they turned and made their way to the car, Melissa unlocked the doors, and they both got in.

Amelia felt the cold and shivered. Seeing Amelia shiver and hearing her breath catch. Melissa popped the trunk, stepped out of the car, and got something out of the trunk. She brought back a light blanket. She gave it to Amelia saying, "it gets really cool here, even during the hottest part of summer. It's the conjunction of the wind off the ocean, the setting sun, and the breeze as it speeds up the river."

"Wow, talk about being prepared," Amelia joked, but was thankful. She shivered because the temperature had dropped, but also her body was betraying her and warming her from within. Plus, she was quite nervous to be with Melissa, in a car, parked in the dark.

"Well, I had better take you home now," Melissa said as she

turned onto Hwy 30, and headed for Charleston. Then made the turn toward North Charleston, to take Amelia home.

They were both quiet on the way back, unsure what to say. Amelia was thinking about the turmoil in her heart and mind concerning the feelings she was having for Melissa.

Melissa was thinking of the feelings she had for Amelia, scared she might say or do something that would scare Amelia away. So, she kept silent as they listened to soft jazz on the radio.

"I hope you really enjoyed today," Melissa said, as they turned onto Amelia's street.

"I loved today. Now, I have a new favorite place to watch sunsets from," Amelia said, emotion noticeable in her voice.

"Would you like to come in for a drink?" Amelia asked, not knowing why she had said that.

"I don't think so, it's getting late," Melissa said, knowing if she went in, she would not be able to control herself.

"I understand Melissa, thank you for a wonderful day. I'll see you on Monday," Amelia said, as Melissa pulled into her driveway, and she got out.

"See you on Monday," Melissa said, as the door closed, and she watched Amelia unlock her front door. She backed the car out. What she didn't see is Amelia leaning on the back of the closed door, wondering why she was feeling so much turmoil. Then she opened the door, walked to the mailbox and there was another red envelope waiting. Opening it as soon as she got in the house, it read,

"Your eyes speak to me of yearning. Your heart speaks to me of love. Your body speaks to me of passion. Tomorrow is the day, seize it, be bold, chose your destiny."

On the way home, Melissa could only think about how she

felt about Amelia. She would have to get her emotions in check, otherwise she believed she would scare Amelia away forever. It scared her, and she tried to shake it away, but to no avail.

Arriving home, and entering her home, Melissa's mind kept thinking about how Amelia looked standing on the deck of the lighthouse.

Her hair blown by the breeze, her cheeks flushed from the climb, and her eyes alight marveling at the sight they looked at. Her heart ached to take Amelia in her arms, but she thought that would never happen.

'How could I let this happen to me?' Melissa questioned herself, as she walked into the bathroom, turned on the shower and began to undress.

The powerful shower drowned out her thoughts for a minute or two, but they returned stronger than before. She just didn't know where to go from here. Tears of want and need streaking down her cheeks.

CHAPTER 15

A week passed, and Amelia received no letter. The weekend came and went, then when she got home on Monday after work, there was another letter. She decided not to open it until the next morning because she was tired and just wanted to go to bed.

The next morning, Amelia opened the red envelope, took out the letter, and noticed there was more than a sentence or two. She read it aloud to herself,

"I have seen the light in your eyes and know there is light in your heart. Keep your heart open, to be able to feel true love. Make every moment count. Look away from timidness and embrace boldness. Win heart and love in the process."

As she read it, the message was loud and clear. It was time to shy away from the girl she had been and become the women she should be.

It would be a while before she could truly embrace the feelings in her heart. But she knew she had begun to change.

Weeks passed, and Amelia's life continued happily. Every day she was able to help someone, which helped her confidence. But she was troubled.

At night, she could only think of Melissa. After weeks of emotional turmoil, she decided to see what her feelings were all about. Letting go of preconceived notions, and allowing herself to act on her feelings would hopefully give her the courage she needed to talk to Melissa. Right or wrong, she would take the first step and see where it would lead.

The more she thought about it at night, the more she

realized she had deep feelings for Melissa. She had no idea where they came from, but she felt like she needed to explore them. If she could only get out of her own head and let her heart lead.

At home, she continued to receive the red envelopes and letters, and Amelia's heart soared every time she received one. *"Have you decided to put preconceived notions aside and allow love in? Love answers all questions, solves all problems. Let true love in."*

"Will you receive me with love in your heart, or doubts on your mind? Answer the question. If you believe in love...let true love guide you from now until eternity."

"What would you say to me now if you knew who I was? Would you tell me you love me? Your heart knows who I am, there should be no question."

Then one day, during a particularly difficult day, when one of her clients had been taken to the hospital by ambulance after a brutal attack by her ex, Amelia broke down.

She had been struggling lately, with the turmoil in her heart about Melissa. Then with her client being assaulted, it just broke her emotional bubble.

She sat in her office, with the door closed, and her chair turned toward the wall. Her mind churning a mile a minute, and tears falling down her cheeks uncontrollably.

She jumped a little when she heard her office door open and close. She had not realized someone had knocked twice. She quickly wiped tears away. Then she turned her chair around to see who was entering.

Melissa was there, staring at her, concern on her face. "Are you okay? What's happened?" Melissa asked walking around the desk, seeing Amelia crying, as she began walking toward her.

Amelia stood up and turned towards her credenza to get a tissue. Answering with a shaky voice, she said, "Kelly Carter was attacked by her ex a few hours ago. She's in the hospital. I thought her struggle was all over. How could he do this to her, after all this time?"

"Oh Amelia, I'm so sorry. Kelly is so nice; I just can't believe he did this. I thought he was in jail?" Melissa asked, feeling Amelia's despondence.

"He only served 6 months of his 10-month sentence. They released him early on good behavior. That's ironic isn't it, good behavior?" Amelia said, skepticism in her voice, along with a touch of hurt. Her voice was catching as she continued to cry. Memories flooded her from her own experience. The pain was visceral with every moment that passed.

"I know Amelia. That's the hardest part of my job. We give these women so much hope when their abusers are finally put away. Then, the justice system does its thing and lets us down. It's disheartening, I know from first-hand knowledge." Melissa finished as she approached Amelia.

Amelia felt Melissa near her and turned to her. Without thinking, Melissa put her arms around Amelia and hugged her, trying to comfort her. Amelia hugged Melissa back, feeling her arms around her. Then she put her head on Melissa's shoulder and cried into her neck. The sobbing and emotion flowed. It was minutes before they began to ebb.

Melissa whispered, "It's going to be all right Amelia. Just let it all out," as she rubbed Amelia's back. They stood there for a few minutes, then Melissa felt Amelia stir in her arms.

Melissa eased her hold on Amelia, thinking Amelia wanted her to let go. Melissa took half a step back, partially releasing

Amelia. But when Melissa went to look at Amelia's face, to see how she was doing, Amelia leaned forward and kissed Melissa.

The kiss took Melissa by surprise. Her mind wanted her to pull away, but her body said no. Melissa took a deep breath, without releasing Amelia's lips, and deepened the kiss. All the need, desire, and waiting had taken its toll on Melissa. She wanted Amelia to feel what she felt. Holding her in her arms and kissing her over, and over again. Each time her tongue explored, wanting to fulfill the desire her body was feeling.

Amelia's phone rang, bringing them both back to reality. Realizing what she had done, Melissa released Amelia and started, "Oh Amelia, I'm so sorry. I can't believe I did that. I'm so embarrassed. Please forgive me. I didn't mean for that to happen," Melissa stammered as she took another step back, turned around and ran out of Amelia's office, leaving Amelia standing there dazed.

Amelia knew she had reacted to Melissa trying to make her feel better. She knew it was not Melissa that initiated the kiss. 'It was me,' Amelia thought to herself. 'I'm the one that initiated.'

The whole thing hit Amelia head on, the fact she had broken down. The fact that she had kissed Melissa. The fact that Melissa had run out of the office.

So much emotion hit Amelia at one time, she went into her bathroom, closed the door, and let it all out. Crying for what seemed like hours. Then she finally stopped, washed her face, and left the bathroom.

She walked to her desk, typed a letter of resignation, and emailed it to Melissa. Then she walked out of the office. She jotted down instructions for her assistants and put them on the communications board. Then she left the building, walked to her car, and headed home.

Crying all the way home, she knew now she was in love with Melissa. But she also knew Melissa blamed herself. How could she straighten all of this out?

When she arrived home, she didn't even check her mailbox, but ran inside, to her bedroom and cried until she fell asleep.

CHAPTER 16

Amelia had turned her phone off, not wanting to talk to anyone. She had shut herself off from the outside world. She cried at night, felt like a zombie during the day. Day after day, she wished she knew what to do. She had not received any more letters either, so she was sure they were from Melissa. Those letters had meant everything to Amelia. But now they were useless to her.

A week later, sitting on her back deck, sipping on a glass of wine, she heard the doorbell ring. She heard it ring again and again, as she walked toward the front door.

When she answered the door, Kim Brooks was standing there. Seeing Kim standing there took Amelia by surprise.

"Amelia, so glad you answered the door. I've been calling you every day. But either your phone is broken, or you haven't been answering. Can I come in and talk to you," Kim said, as Amelia opened the door wider to let Kim in.

"What can I do for you Kim? Why are you here?" Amelia asked in rapid succession.

"I want you to know that Melissa and I are not accepting your letter of resignation. You take as much time as you need, then come back to work." Kim said, trying to gauge what Amelia was feeling and thinking.

"I can't work there anymore. It's too painful," Amelia said. Tears welling in her eyes, as she turned away from Kim.

"I know emotions run high with our clients. We can't be there to protect them 24/7. We can only do what the law allows us. And I know we are human, and I know that it is painful and hurtful when our clients suffer at someone else's hand. It is something I struggle with every day. But I know how much worse it could be if we weren't there for them," Kim said, as she removed her coat, and sat on the couch, watching Amelia closely.

"I know, it just makes me feel helpless," Amelia said. Her emotions showed on her face.

"I understand, you and Melissa had words," Kim said, continuing to read Amelia's face.

"Oh, we had more than words. I kissed her when she was trying to comfort me about a client," Amelia said, continuing to avoid Kim's eyes on her. "I know that was wrong. I know emotions were running high. I don't know what came over me. But I'm embarrassed, and I embarrassed Melissa. The one thing I didn't want was to hurt Melissa," Amelia said, anguish in voice.

"The way Melissa tells it, she was the one who initiated it. Is that right?" Kim asked, wanting to know the truth, and suspecting Amelia had deep feelings for Melissa.

"No. I'm the one who initiated it. She was so comforting as she hugged me. My body responded, and I lost my head. I'm the one that kissed her first, she just returned the kiss. I'm the one that ruined our friendship. I can't forgive myself," Amelia said, her breath catching as she explained.

"Did you ever stop to think, that maybe, both of you have feelings for each other," Kim asked, knowing the truth.

"Melissa has been nothing but professional, caring, and thoughtful. She gave me no signs she had feelings for me, none that I noticed anyway, unless I missed some signals. You know this is all new to me," Amelia's voice pleaded.

"Well, I think you should talk to Melissa. It does no good

for you to run away from each other. You must talk to each other, and find out for sure how you feel, how Melissa feels," Kim said, knowing Melissa blamed herself, and was despondent at losing Amelia. But Kim had decided to try to get them to talk to each other.

"I can't. I need time. I need to decide what I really want. Please tell Melissa not to blame herself. Tell her I really care about her, but I need time to figure everything out. I'm sorry Kim, I know I've left both of you at a busy time," Amelia said, feeling sorry for her quick resignation. But, at the time, she thought it was the right thing to do.

"Look, the longer you wait, the worse it's going to get. Go to Melissa, talk it out. You might find that you have more in common than you think. Please do this for me?" Kim encouraged, but saw no response from Amelia, her shoulders heaving as she cried.

"In time. I just can't right now. It hurts too much," Amelia said, as she walked to her bedroom and slammed the door. Throwing herself on the bed, she cried until her head hurt.

Amelia heard the door close, as Kim left the house, walked to her car, then left. Amelia began to realize her last connection to Melissa had ended. Now she was all alone again.

CHAPTER 17

Months had passed since Amelia had resigned. She had gone back to night classes, but resisted the urge to walk the campus, thinking she might see Melissa again. She was still too hurt to let that happen. She had received no more red envelopes and letters. She was sure they had been from Melissa.

She had decided to work from home during the day. She was helping the women's and family shelter gather resources to expand their offering. The phone and computer during the day, and classes at night kept Amelia busy.

But she was not busy enough to keep her mind wandering to thoughts of Melissa. She remembered the kiss they had shared, and how it brought such yearning. Each time, Amelia quelled her thoughts and needs, keeping herself busy.

Then, one Saturday, when the temperature had climbed high enough, and tired of being cooped up in her house, Amelia decided to head for Sullivan's Island to walk. It was a beautiful Saturday, and she wanted to take advantage of the great weather.

She put on her favorite sneakers, yoga pants, and sweatshirt. Put a small cooler with water and ice in the trunk of her car and headed for the beach on Sullivan's Island.

Twenty minutes later she had parked her car, grabbed her water bottle, and was walking on the beach. She headed for Murrel's Inlet; a walk she had done a thousand times before. There were people on the beach, and she watched the children run in the water, then out onto the sand, with smiles on their faces, and glee in their squeals of joy.

Arriving at Murrel's Inlet, Amelia took a seat on a clump of sea grass. Looking down at the sand, then at the sea, her mind brought back the kiss on the fateful day.

She closed her eyes, so she could remember every detail. She remembered the feel of Melissa's arms around her. She remembered the smell of Melissa's perfume on her neck. She remembered Melissa's voice, trying to comfort her. She remembered Melissa's gaze, as she had looked at her before the kiss. She remembered the warmth and tenderness in the kiss. Then she remembered the passion she had felt rise within, as Melissa had deepened the kiss.

With her eyes still closed, she swore she smelled Melissa's perfume now. She opened her eyes, and there she stood. Melissa's eyes riveted on Amelia.

"What are you doing here?" Amelia asked. Her heart was throbbing in her chest.

"I've been walking here every Saturday since you left, waiting for you. Your phone kept going to voicemail, and I just couldn't leave a message. I didn't think I should go to your house, after Kim's visit. So, I just waited. Eventually, I knew you would walk your favorite beach." Melissa said, never taking her eyes off Amelia.

"I don't know what to say, Melissa. I'm the one that kissed you first. I know I embarrassed you. I'm sorry. I'm sorry you blamed yourself. I just don't want you to blame yourself anymore. You did nothing wrong." Amelia said, knowing she was at fault. Looking down at her hands, she did not see the emotion on Melissa's face.

"Amelia, tell me how you feel about me?" Melissa said, hoping.

"Melissa, honestly, I think I'm I love with you. But my emotions have been in turmoil for so long, I just can't be sure anymore." Amelia started crying. Deep down she knew she was still in love with Melissa.

Without hesitation Melissa said, "Amelia, I think I have been in love with you since the first day I met you. It scares me how deeply I feel for you. Your kiss meant more to me than you could ever know. I was afraid I had scared you away. I was supposed to be a professional. I was supposed to be the one in control. But I failed me and you that day. That's why I ran away." Melissa eyes welled with tears.

Amelia heard the words, and her heart raced. "Melissa, this is all new to me and it scares the hell out of me. I've never been in love with anyone. I married Mark, because at the time he made me feel good about myself. But we both know where that ended."

Amelia continued, "With you I feel safe, cared for, wanted, and loved. But I've never felt like this before. I'm scared to admit to myself that this is what I want. I'm scared of being hurt again. Can you understand that?"

"Amelia, stand up and look at me," Melissa asked. Her gaze never leaving Amelia's eyes.

Amelia did as Melissa asked.

"Stand there and look me in the eyes and tell me how you feel." Melissa said, gazing deeply into Amelia's eyes.

Amelia hesitated a moment, then said with a quiver in her throat, "Melissa I'm in love with you."

Melissa opened her arms, and Amelia stepped into them. Melissa whispered, "Amelia, I'm in love with you too. No more running away." Their arms tightened around each other.

"I know this is new to you. I want us to take things slow,

so we can learn everything about each other. So, we can learn to communicate with each other. No more running away. No more denying how we feel. But moving at a pace that makes us both comfortable. How does that sound?" Melissa asked emotionally. One hand on Amelia's back, the other at Amelia's neck.

Amelia raised her head off Melissa's shoulder, turned and kissed Melissa with all the emotion and passion she was feeling. Melissa returned the kiss with her entire being.

Gasping for air, they both chuckled, "I bet we look like college students stealing away," Melissa laughed lightly, watching Amelia's face looking at her.

"Well, you know I am currently in college, so that term actually applies," Amelia said joking, seeking Melissa's lips again, kissing lightly this time, luxuriating in the tenderness of the kiss and the comfort of her arms.

Afterwards, they walked the beach, talking, and kissing for a while, before the sun started to go down and they had to leave.

CHAPTER 18

Melissa and Amelia dated for 3 months before they decided to get physical. They had discussed it since it would be their first time with each other. They wanted it to be special.

They planned a 4-day weekend at Sullivan's Island. They rented a condo, which opened to a magnificent balcony facing the ocean.

They went sightseeing the first day, did a little shopping, had seafood for dinner, then got back to the condominium before dark.

They lit candles, poured wine, and turned on soft jazz that echoed through the condominium. They took their time, sitting on the couch listening to the music, talking about their day, trading kisses, and gently touching each other. They listened to the music playing and the waves crashing. Slowly their kisses deepened, passion building between them.

When the time was right, Melissa took Amelia's hand, and they walked into the bathroom. After turning the shower on, they slowly undressed each other, gasping as they saw each other's beautiful bodies for the first time. Then they entered the shower together.

Melissa wrapped her arms around Amelia's waist, pulling her in so their bodies molded to each other. The shower water cascading down their bodies. Then, Amelia wrapped her arms around Melissa's neck, kissing her jaw line to her mouth. They kissed deeply. Both moaning, their feelings for each other heard in their guttural sounds.

"I want you," Melissa then whispered in Amelia's ear. She reached between their bodies and lowered her hand to Amelia's mound. Slowly, she flicked her fingers through the slit, finding Amelia's throbbing clit and her opening.

Continuing to kiss Amelia, Melissa entered Amelia, while holding her against the shower wall. Then as Amelia gasped, Melissa whispered in her ear, "I have wanted you for so long," and Amelia whispered back, "I have waited for you for so long."

As Melissa inserted her second finger, she felt Amelia's body respond by tilting her pelvis. Melissa felt Amelia's body spasm as she started to pump her fingers in and out. Slow at first, then quicker as Melissa felt Amelia nearing climax. Their kisses became deeper and more enthusiastic. Bodies in rhythm, Melissa brought Amelia to climax. Amelia almost collapsed from the intensity. Melissa continued the rhythm of her fingers, drawing out the climax, until Amelia was totally spent.

Minutes later, they exited the shower, dried off, and Melissa led Amelia to the king size bed. Looking deeply into her eyes, Melissa asked Amelia to lay on her back on the king-size bed. Then Melissa slowly trailed kisses from Amelia's ankles to her thighs, her pubic mound, her hips and waist. Then, she engulfed Amelia's right nipple. Working it in her mouth, Melissa moaned as Amelia arched her back. Melissa placed her right hand on Amelia's waist pulling her even closer. Melissa put her leg between Amelia's legs, feeling her warmth and wetness.

Switching to Amelia's left breast, Melissa used her teeth to stimulate the nipple into contracting. At the same time, Amelia gasped, then deeply moaned. Amelia's hands entwined in Melissa's hair, encouraging her to take it one step further. At the same time, Melissa's left hand had entwined in Amelia's right hand moving it above her head.

After a minute or two, Melissa let go of her hand and got up on all fours. Her gaze communicated what she was going to do next.

Slowly, Melissa crawled down the bed, and kissed Amelia's pubic area. Amelia knew what was coming next and opened her legs wide for Melissa. Melissa gazed lovingly and passionately at Amelia as she lowered her head to Amelia's clit. Amelia entwined her fingers in Melissa's hair, pushing her head closer.

Using her tongue, Melissa flicked the engorged clit and Amelia gasped. Then she slowly separated Amelia's folds with her tongue, licking from just under the clit to the opening, repeating her actions time and time again.

Amelia's hips raised off the mattress of their own volition. Her legs quivering as passion took over. Slowly and methodically, Melissa continued to engulf Amelia's clit, flicked it with her tongue, then licked her way to Amelia's opening. Repeating the rhythm of her tongue, Melissa then surprised Amelia by inserting two fingers.

Amelia's gasp of delight and ecstasy reverberated through the room, as her body arched off the bed. "Oh Melissa" she whispered, her voice trembling at the approaching climax. Melissa began to slowly pump in and out of Amelia, while her tongue engulfed and sucked on Amelia's clit.

Amelia's body spasmed, as she began to climax. Melissa then moved her mouth from Amelia's clit to her opening, drinking in Amelia's juices as they exited her body. Their vocal moans and groans conveying both their pleasure.

Melissa's hands then went back to Amelia's breasts, kneading them, as her mouth continued the exploration of Amelia's body from her mound back to her mouth. Amelia responded with another guttural moan of delight and ecstasy.

Melissa then kissed Amelia, wrapping her in her arms, allowing Amelia to taste herself on Melissa's lips. Repeatedly, they kissed deeply, using their tongues to explore the outline of each other's lips, and each other's tongues and mouths. Amelia extracting every single drop of herself from Melissa's mouth.

As they gasped for air, Amelia spoke softly to Melissa, "please let me touch you." Melissa nodded, then laid down on the bed, and Amelia got on top.

Amelia kissed Melissa's mouth, then planted kisses along her jawline to her ear. Then she worked her way from Melissa's ear to her collar, and slowly to the right breast. Engulfing Melissa's nipple, she used her teeth and tongue. Melissa moaned with exquisite passion as her body responded to Amelia.

Then Amelia lowered her hand to Melissa's mound and let her fingers explore. Melissa groaned and raised her hips, encouraging Amelia to enter her. But Amelia was not in a hurry. She wanted to feel Melissa's body respond to her touch.

Amelia used her fingers to separate Melissa's folds. Then she followed the folds to Melissa's entrance. Amelia teased Melissa by inserting the tip of her finger, then extracting it. Again and again, she repeated the action. "You are driving me crazy," Melissa said, her voice straining against the rising tide of her passion, as her legs quivered.

Then Amelia inserted two fingers and began to pump, as she lowered her head to Melissa's clit. Flicking it with her tongue, she felt Melissa's back arch, reacting to Amelia's actions.

"Oh Amelia, look at what you do to me," Melissa whispered, as her body reacted to what Amelia was doing. Quickly, Melissa reached her climax. Her body jerking and spasming, releasing the passion that had built up since the first time she had met Amelia.

Amelia kept pumping and licking, drawing out Melissa's climax. Then she slowly extracted her fingers and crawled up to kiss Melissa. Melissa kissed her, tasting herself on Amelia's lips. They kissed repeatedly, as their bodies continued to react to the passion between them. Legs entwined, hands entwined, mounds grinding, passions flaring. Over and over through the night they brought each other to climaxes.

Each day, they would explore outside, then they would return to the condominium to explore each other. Kissing, lovemaking, touching, and so much more. Heightened awareness as passions flared. They continued to satisfy each other's needs. Their joy and happiness were visible on their faces.

Time passed too quickly. They knew 4 days would not be enough. But they also knew they had a lifetime to live, love, and dream.

CHAPTER 19

Two years have passed, and their lives had changed for the better. Melissa and Kim's law practice has grown, and now they have six attorneys and six more support staff assisting them. Two of the new attorneys were Melissa's former co-workers from the DA's office, who decided to join her, in her mission to provide women and families advocacy and support.

Kim and Robin had their first child and are ecstatic. As is Melissa, now the godmother to a little brown-haired, brown-eyed child that is beloved by all.

Melissa and Amelia have moved in together into a new home on Sullivan's Island. They are having a party this Saturday to celebrate their two-year anniversary, and their new home.

Melissa has bought an engagement ring, and plans to ask Amelia to marry her, while they are visiting the lighthouse on Sunday afternoon at sunset. She is sure Amelia will say yes. She also hopes to have the wedding there too. And, she has a final love letter she will give Amelia on their wedding day.

What Melissa doesn't know is that by accident, Amelia has found out what Melissa's plans are and has bought Melissa an engagement ring too; and will surprise her at the same time. She also has bundled the love letters Melissa sent her and is going to present them to her as a promise of her forever love at their wedding.

They both know what the future holds for them, and every time they walk Sullivan's Island, where they live now, they are walking back into each other's arms, sharing love, and sharing dreams.

THE LOVE LETTERS

"You are beautiful! God has granted you true beauty beginning from the inside and showing on the outside. Your heart is pure, for when you love, you will love with all your heart."

"God made you the way you are. Perfect in every way. Pure heart, clear mind, intelligent, and faith filled."

"Inner strength and courage are yours when life becomes difficult. Let your faith, friends, and special ones give you their guidance so you can find what you are looking for."

"Life begins, love begins, dreams begin."

"Dream of living, dream of loving, nothing is beyond you. You are free to find your future, define your life, and to explore love. Dream your dreams."

"Love comes from the heart, listen to your heart. Too often we allow our minds to stop listening, but our hearts know what they want."

"When you least expect it love will find you. Will you be brave enough to recognize it."

"Living life to its fullest, accepting everyday as it comes, allows love to grow in your heart."

"Don't let preconceived notions about love guide your heart. Your heart is pure, it only knows real love and kindness. Let it feel."

"The face of love may be obscured, but the reality of love is clear. Do not try to hide from it, let it come in."

"Open your heart, open your mind, your future is here. Opportunities knock but once. Whether love or work, neither will wait."

"Acquaintances to friends to lovers, open your heart, see more. Let your heart rule; as your mind may be confused, but your heart always knows the truth."

"Soon, a new opportunity will lead you to eventual happiness and love. Your mind may not recognize it, but your heart will. Accept it!"

"Do you see what I see when you look in the mirror...a pure heart ready to share its love. Open your heart to all the possibilities; love is there, prepare your heart."

"Passion, love, longing...all related to that feeling in your heart. Open your heart, open your mind, feel it!"

"Every heart knows when it is in love; the difference is quieting the doubts in our minds."

"Your eyes speak to me of yearning. Your heart speaks to me of love. Your body speaks to me of passion. Tomorrow is the day, seize it, be bold, chose your destiny."

"I have seen the light in your eyes and know there is light in your heart. Keep your heart open, to be able to feel true love. Make every moment count. Look away from timidness and embrace boldness. Win heart and love in the process."

"Have you decided to put preconceived notions aside and allow love in? Love answers all questions, solves all problems. Let true love in."

"Will you receive me with love in your heart, or doubts on your mind? Answer the question. If you believe in love...let true love guide you from now until eternity."

"What would you say to me now if you knew who I was? Would you tell me you love me? Your heart knows who I am, there should be no question."

THE LOVE LETTER FROM
Melissa to Amelia

My beloved Amelia.

    I have waited a lifetime for you. My dreams brought you to me but then took you away. Needing to hold you, needing to kiss you, needing to love you, my head and heart have ached for you.

    Our beginning was blind, but we are blind no more. I see all the love, passion, and desire in your eyes. I know you see all the love, passion, and desire in mine.

    Our future is bright, just like the light beaming out onto the ocean. As the light searches the ocean and finds its target, we have searched for love and found it.

    So, let us live our lives together forevermore. Living each day to its fullest. Comforted by the knowledge that our love is pure. That we have finally found what we were looking for... each other.

    Yours Forevermore, Melissa

THE LOVE LETTER FROM
Amelia to Melissa

My true love Melissa,

I have waited a lifetime for you. First you freed me from my pain and suffering. Then you showed me how to open my heart to real love.

I have learned to feel all the love, passion, and desire you have for me, and I have for you. I feel it in my heart, see it with my eyes, desire it in my mind and body.

I dream of our future, filled with love, passion, and desire. Our love lighting the way to our future together, finally finding what we searched for our entire lives.

Let us live each day to its fullest, from now until the end. Knowledge of pure love fills us and provides for us. That love lets us know that we have finally found what we have been looking for...each other.

With all my love forever, Amelia

THANK YOU

Thank you for reading ***The Love Letters to Amelia***. Maggie Medina is the pen name of Maria M. Medina.

This is my 4th book, after the **Carolina Lesbian Romance Series**: *Edisto Beach Love, Charleston Surrender, and Myrtle Beach Passion*, all inspired by trips to favorite South Carolina cities.

I was born in Puerto Rico, but my dad was in the Army, and we traveled the world. I have lived in Augusta, Georgia for over 50 years, with my wife Pat and our dogs, Abby and Sandy.

We travel often, enjoy great food, and love entertaining. But we also enjoy relaxing in our dream home, listening to music, reading good books, watching our favorite shows on television, sitting by the fireplace, and like visiting with family.

You can reach me at
mariamedinaromances@gmail.com

Made in the USA
Monee, IL
20 February 2025

12444405R00069